I0452235

THE EASTER EGG ENNUI

A LORA WEAVER MYSTERY NOVELLA

KATY LEEN

ISBN: print : 978-1-9990767-4-0

Cover design: Team KL

Cover illustration by Adrienne Alexander

Cover background icons: The Noun Project, Easter basket #7653473

For my own Easter Bunny,
who showed me that every Easter basket
is full if it's assembled with love.

I WOULD HAVE been out the door free and clear five minutes earlier if it weren't for the Easter lilies.

The lilies reigned, bouquet style, from a giant gold vase atop the fireplace mantel in my bff's aunt Claudette's living room. My bff, Camille Caron, stood near the fireplace fiddling with something in a bag, and as I waited for her to stop fiddling, the lilies drew me over with their perky yellow petals and frisky fresh fragrance.

I fingered a silky lily petal and eyed the slew of jetsam surrounding the reigning bouquet. Cookie boxes, nail polish jars, beer bottles, cigarette packs, electronic gizmos, and various other odds and ends crowded together like royal subjects worshipping the majesty of the lilies. Or guards protecting them.

Leaning in for a closer look, I saw each item was labeled with someone's name, all printed in the same blocky handwriting.

"What's with all the mishmash on your aunt's mantel?" I asked Camille.

"Lent offerings," Camille said, like it was obvious.

"*Mignon?*" I said, reading one of the names aloud and reaching for a pile of stubby, brown, gummy sticks bundled and trussed with twine like a miniature stock of firewood. "*Mignon* is doing Lent?"

Camille turned to a sheet of labels sitting on the coffee table, peeled off a sticker, slapped it on the side of a tub of peanut butter, and added the tub to the mantel.

"*Bien sûr, Mignon aussi.*" Camille drew closer to the mirror hanging over the mantel and peered over a bottle of perfume and a box of cookies. She smoothed her short blonde hair and pinched the fins up on the collar of her blouse. "To *tante* Claudette, *Mignon* is family. Everyone who's family does Lent and gives up something."

My eyes trailed over to Claudette's white miniature poodle sprawled on a floor pillow in the corner, his tiny white paws clutching a tan stick so it stood upright, just tall enough for his tiny white teeth to gnaw on the top end.

"Umm. I think maybe *Mignon* didn't get the Lent memo."

Camille looked over at the dog. "*Voyons*, Lora. That stick is chicken flavor." She tapped the mini bundle of sticks in my hand. "These are beef."

I put the sticks back and pointed to the peanut butter with Camille's name plastered over the brand logo. "And you're giving up peanut butter? You don't even like peanut butter."

She shrugged.

"Not that I'm Catholic," I said, "but I thought the point of Lent was to give up something hard. Like a habit you wish you could change or something you love, to show sacrifice or something." I picked up one of the beer bottles. "Like this guy." I read the name off the handwritten label. "Bruno. What? A cousin of yours? He's giving up beer. That's got to be hard."

"Bruno's a pro athlete. He's in training. Bruno never drinks beer when he's in training."

I moved on to one of the cigarette packages. "Okay. Well, what about Solonge here? She's giving up smoking. That's a major addiction. That's definitely hard."

"Solonge never had a cigarette in her life. She has asthma."

I looked down the procession of mantel offerings, noticing the mirror above registered far less of my petite reflection than it had of Camille's taller one. Barely my forehead and the crown of my amber mass of hair showed. Nothing lower, from my blue eyes to my long knit sweater to my tan leggings. Not even when I tried spying between the cookies and cosmetics and got waylaid when I spotted a mini bag of corn chips behind a comic book and wondered if snitching something from someone's stash was a Lent no-no.

"Are you telling me none of these contributions on the mantel are real?" I asked. "What's the point then?"

"*Oui, oui*, they're all real to *tante* Claudette," Camille assured me. "Every year she makes the whole family do Lent. It's very important. She wants everyone to put a symbol here to show we are giving up something. We want to make her happy, so we go along. And we only put things we're willing to go without. Except the kids. It's the kids who put the cookies and nail polish. Sometimes they cheat. It's hard to go without cookies and nail polish for six weeks."

"You mean their sacrifices are really things they like?"

"Sure. They're kids. They're afraid of *tante* Claudette. They think she's got magic powers, like maybe she can talk to God or the Holy Ghost. They heard English kids call *Saint-Esprit* the Holy Ghost and now they think the Holy Ghost is something scary."

Well, yeah. Totally understandable. Tack on the word "ghost" to anything and it sounds scary. Even to me at the tender age of thirty-one. I'm still scared of ghosts. And truth be told I agreed with the kids about Claudette, too. I'd gotten to know her a while back when she and her sister, Camille's mom, had a falling out. I liked Claudette. And her little poodle *Mignon,* who I'd bonded with during a short time he'd bunked at my house. Like everyone in Camille's family I'd met since I'd moved from New York to Montréal over two years ago and Camille and I had become friends, Claudette was kind and welcoming to me. And she even let me visit *Mignon* on my own now and then. But Claudette had also read my tea leaves and scared the bejeebees out of me with her predictions, some of which had come true. Magic powers may be pushing it, but if she could see more than meets the average eye in a bunch of soggy tea leaves, probably indulging her Lent plan was wise. Especially since she also had a reserved pew at the local church, so the talking to God thing wasn't far fetched, either.

Camille motioned through the living room doorway to my shoulder bag where I'd left it on a bench in Claudette's entry hall. "*Et puis,* what did *you* bring?"

"Excuse me?" I said. When Camille told me we'd be stopping by her aunt's house on the way to dinner, she'd said nothing about Lent, let alone me participating. Camille had a family big enough to mount its own travelling *Cirque du Soleil.* She was always stopping by this place or that, dropping things off, picking things up, checking on things when someone was out of town. That's how things worked in her clan. I didn't think to question another stop-by.

Camille reached for the sheet of sticker labels and held it up to me. Few labels remained so it was easy to spot my name somewhere in the middle.

Tiny shivers set my neck atingle.

"I don't have anything for the mantel," I mouthed like Claudette might overhear and race into the room crossing herself or something. Totally irrational I knew, unless she'd cloned herself. Claudette's house was a bungalow with a basement room where she was currently presiding over a church group meeting about Easter. Even through the closed basement door, I could hear the murmur of voices still clucking away led by Claudette.

Which got me thinking something else. "She won't really notice will she?" I asked Camille. "I mean, didn't Lent start weeks ago? Isn't it almost over? Easter's barely a week away. Isn't it a little late to add offerings to the mantel?"

"*Mais non*. It's not late for me. Claudette knows Laurent and me were in Québec City on a case. She expects we followed Lent there. Adding to the mantel is just a formality for Laurent and me."

Laurent was Camille's brother and owned and ran *Investigations C&C*, a PI agency, along with Camille. Making them both my co-bosses, since I was currently training for my license to become a PI and working as their assistant while I earned my stripes. For the few weeks they'd been away, most of that assisting had me hunkered down at the office doing boring phone reconnaissance and computer checks. And helping the receptionist Arielle, aka Claudette's daughter, make tie-breaking decisions between items in her online shopping carts. Extracurricular shopping clearly not being Arielle's Lent offering. Lent didn't seem high on Arielle's list at all since she flew the coop days ago and was currently sunning herself in some far off land with her boyfriend, Jason.

"But late for you?" Camille went on to say with the hint of a smile. "*Peut-être. Tante* Claudette knows you stayed *au bureau* with Arielle."

"That's so not fair," I said. "I didn't even know I was supposed to participate. I'm not even Catholic. Claudette knows that."

"You think that matters? Family. That's what matters and you're practically family." She swung her arm towards *Mignon*. "You think *le petit là* had a baptism?"

5

I cut my eyes to the dog. It wouldn't surprise me actually. It wouldn't surprise me at all to find a doggy-sized, frou-frou baptism gown tucked into a box in one of Claudette's closets.

But gown or not, she really did treat *Mignon* like family, and I was flattered to be in his company. Flattered and the hint of another feeling. Something I hadn't felt in quite a while, since my parents had passed away and I'd been left with little family of my own. I was feeling an edge of family-style guilt at the thought of disappointing Claudette.

"Well, I've got nothing," I said, scanning the mantel, looking for inspiration. An idea hit and I went to fetch my purse. "Here." I pulled out a half-eaten slab of chocolate. "I've got this. Will this work?"

Camille looked at the chocolate like it was on fire. A mix of shock and fear radiating from her eyes like lighthouse beams shooting out to sea in the dead of night.

She snatched the bar from me. "*T'es folle?* You can't give up chocolate!"

I snatched the bar back. "Sure I can. It's only for a few days." I folded the extra wrapper bits under and used the label with my name on it to seal the ends shut. I placed it among the other jetsam, leaning it against one of the beer bottles so my name was clearly visible. "There. Now let's get out of here and go to dinner like we were supposed to before you ambushed me with this side trip to Lent land." I headed for the front door to put on my shoes. "Next thing I know you'll be telling me I have to fast on Good Friday, too."

Camille shot me her "but of course" Frenchwoman look. The one that made it seem not only obvious but ridiculous for me to even consider *not* fasting. I was beginning to think if we didn't leave Claudette's house soon, by the end of the week I really would be Catholic.

. . .

I WAS OUT Claudette's front door and on her porch before Camille even had her jacket on, my exodus stopped short when I ran into Laurent on his way up the porch steps. His eyes almost black against the backdrop of dimming blue, spring evening sky, his dark hair disheveled, wisps fluttering with the breeze and drifting to his chin. He had on dark jeans and a slice of white shirt hit me eye level, peeking out from his grey tailored overcoat.

He stood a moment on the top step then leaned in to kiss my cheeks hello, his usual scruff thickened and leaving lingering warmth on my skin as our greeting ended and café haze from his hair and clothes migrated onto mine.

I groped for the porch railing as we separated. The last time I'd seen Laurent was before he left on the Québec City case. He'd stopped by my house and given me a tiny doll that had shown up during a previous investigation. In an odd turn of events, the doll tied into my mom's past as a teenager. Laurent hadn't said exactly why he'd given me the doll and he didn't need to. We both knew how much connections to my mom meant to me. One of the reasons I moved here stemmed from a desire for that connection. Even though I was raised in New York, my mom had been from Canada and I wanted to get in touch with those Canadian roots and my mom's life before me. The doll definitely qualified as part of the latter. The doll had been handmade in a likeness of my mom. Probably by my mom's own hands. So giving me the doll was a sweet and big gesture. Maybe too big.

The police expected the doll to be handed in as evidence in the investigation, but instead Laurent had given it to me, claiming it as "misplaced." I knew not one cop on the force would buy that. Laurent had a sterling reputation for integrity and exacting expertise. So two days later, as much as I hated to part with it, I turned the doll in claiming it as "found" and pleading mea culpa for its temporary AWOL status. Laurent had gone to Québec City about the same time, and we hadn't spoken about it since. I knew by now he had to know what I'd done, and I was feeling a bit sheepish about it. And apparently a little off-balance at suddenly running into him, which I covered brilliantly with total avoidance of the subject.

"You here about Lent?" I asked him.

He nodded. One hand trailed towards his coat pocket, stopping midway and smoothing fabric.

I smiled. "Nice move. But you're training me to be a PI, remember? I saw you reach for your pocket. Your offering for the mantel collection in there?"

He gave me a non-committal shrug, his eyes barely meeting mine.

Laurent had a way of making himself unreadable. A skill he'd acquired back in his cop days and trotted out whenever it suited him. Since I had a skill of reading people that I'd acquired in my old job as a social worker, him trotting out his skill and thwarting mine rarely suited *me*.

"Ah, c'mon," I said. "I'll show you mine if you show me yours."

This got a smile out of him. A smile that faded quickly at the sound of a bellowing voice behind us.

"*Elle est là*, Camille!"

I turned to the owner of the bellowing voice. Claudette, wearing a flowered housedress, socks midway up her calves, fluffy blue slippers, and a wide smile outlined in smudged red lipstick. The only stitch of makeup on her otherwise scrubbed face framed by silver hair escaping a bun.

"*Elle est là avec* Laurent," Claudette yelled some more, this time into the house.

Camille poked her head out of the doorway and rolled her eyes at me, adding in a raised eyebrow and a head shake. Bff sign language I cobbled together like a cryptogram, deciphering her message to mean something in the neighborhood of "I'm cooked now and have only myself to blame."

"*Et voilà*," Camille whispered to me as I got ushered back into the house by Claudette. "Don't say I didn't try to save you."

Save me? Save me from what?

A tiny flock of older women encircled me, and it occurred to me maybe "save me from whom?" was a better question.

Beyond the cluster of heads surrounding me, I spotted Claudette hauling Laurent in, closing the door, and cornering him behind it, her finger wagging in his face. By the look in her eye and the pace of her finger wag, it looked like maybe I wasn't the only one who needed saving.

I WANTED DESPERATELY to know what was up with Claudette's finger wagging in Laurent's face, but I couldn't hear even snippets of the words going along with the wag. The gaggle of women around me nattered in French, over-speaking one another, looking at me then back to each other and nodding in waves as though they were casting votes by head bobs. Probably I should have been trying to get a beat on their nattering, but I had a hard enough time understanding French coming at me in mono mode, let alone in stereo from a herd of speakers.

So instead I tried to catch Laurent's eye, but his focus was on Claudette, both of them in profile. His body stood firm, his toned muscles holding him in perfect alignment. As usual. No giveaways there. His face, or at least the side of it I could see, stayed neutral, stubble shading his cheeks, hiding subtle tells.

A few of the women surrounding me shifted places, and for a second I got a fuller view of Laurent and Claudette. Her wagging finger had lowered, resting near the side slit pocket of her house-dress, and her face turned my way, making my own cheeks grow instantly hot at the thought of being caught intruding on their aunt-nephew moment. Claudette probably included curiosity as the eighth deadly sin and I was plenty guilty of it.

I had no business poking my nose into their business, yet somehow I couldn't help myself. Maybe it was because Laurent was my boss. Or my mentor. Or the big brother of my best friend. Or because the longer I knew him, the harder I was finding it to figure him out. But seeing him on the receiving end of a finger wag intrigued me.

He looked my way, his gaze fleeting but soft, upping the glow in my cheeks. Then he slipped out the door, leaving my curiosity hanging in the air along with the scents of tea and vanilla that seemed to permanently linger in Claudette's house. And the flock of women who'd apparently taken to lingering around me, looking at me like I was next lamb up on shear day.

2

―――――

"*T*HAT WAS NOTHING," I said to Camille when we finally settled into our seats at a bistro for dinner. "What was with that bit about me needing saving? You had me all worried. You had me thinking the church ladies were sizing me up to give Jesus a baby sister or something. All they wanted was for me to help out with the Sunday school kids and their Easter egg hunt."

Camille tapped the side of her glass, and a waiter appeared and filled the glass with red wine. "*All* they wanted?" she said. "It's a bunch of little kids. With sticky candy hands dragging around sticky baskets. Running and screaming in the park."

I smiled. Camille had a family with oodles of kids she doted on. But she did most of that doting in tiny time increments fixed by the alarm on her phone. And sticky hands were kept at a safe distance.

"Exactly," I said. "What's not to love?"

Truth be told I'd been thrilled to be asked to help by Claudette and was eager to do her proud. Plus, in my old social work days,

I'd done a lot of work with kids and I missed it sometimes, so I was kinda looking forward to contributing to their Easter festivities by dolling out candy eggs.

Camille rolled her eyes at me and signaled the waiter again, this time to take our orders. Both of us getting spaghetti, hers with meatballs, mine without. Both of us taking the accompanying side salads, which came mere minutes later for us to munch on while we waited for the main course.

"*Et,* what about the pageant? All those kids in all those costumes, bumping into each other on the stage and missing their lines." She rolled her eyes again. "*Bien trop pour moi.*"

I dipped a piece of lettuce in dressing set in a cute tiny bowl shaped like a tomato. "What pageant?"

"The pageant for *Pâques.*" A slow smile came to Camille's lips. "The one you agreed to help with at show time? Make sure the kids follow their cues and go out at the right time. Give them their lines if they forget."

My piece of lettuce belly-flopped into the dressing bowl. "I agreed to help with the egg hunt. I didn't agree to help with a pageant."

"*Oui, oui,* you did. Right after you got that awful bracelet from Madame Dumont. You nodded your head so much to everything she said I thought you'd get whiplash."

I set down my fork and checked my wrists, finding a plastic green coiled bracelet tucked up one sweater sleeve, the coils wound like an old telephone cord. I blinked at it, no memory of how it got there, and eased it free from my sweater. Two keys escaped along with the bracelet, the keys dangling from a tiny silver ring tethering them to the bracelet.

"I don't remember anyone giving me this. Which one was Madame Dumont?"

"The one with the eyebrows painted on like doorway arches."

Oh right. If the doorway arches had been scorched with soot. Madame Dumont had the darkest eyebrows I'd ever seen. But maybe that was just in contrast to her nearly translucent white hair and skin. "I remember her. She's the one who kept snapping her fingers at everyone."

"*Oui.* She's the ringleader of *Les Femmes de l'Église* group."

"Really? I thought Claudette would be the head. She practically lives at the church." At least she did when she wasn't reading tea leaves.

"*Pas encore.* She's second in line."

"Second in line?" I laughed. "You make it sound like the throne to England. We're talking about a group of ladies who organize holiday events and throw parish teas."

Camille shook her head. "Events and teas are nothing. It's the prestige. *Et aussi* the film in the works. Next year some big director is making a movie about *le saint frère* André, the guy who started the *Oratoire Saint-Joseph*, the big famous church here near the mountain. The film is going to show his life from his early days to his death to how he became a saint. As some kind of publicity thing, the filmmakers are giving bit roles to all the local church group heads."

"So whoever is the head of *Les Femmes de l'Église* group gets to be in the movie?"

"*Exactement.* To be part of such an important film for a local saint is a big deal to the church ladies. They think it's a way to leave a mark, show a legacy of their own."

Not being the religious type, I wasn't much interested in the movie topic, but I could understand the allure for the church group ladies. Plus, lots of people still got excited about the idea of fifteen minutes of fame. Especially if that fame came in social circles they cared about.

"Well, I guess Madame Dumont is pretty excited about it then."

Camille raised an eyebrow. "A year's a long time. She'd have to keep the head title to qualify for the movie role."

I sat back, swiped my mouth with a napkin, and dropped it in my plate. "You're not suggesting she may get ousted from her "throne" before that, are you? Like the first-in-line lady will stage a coup?"

Camille shrugged. "There's a new election coming after Easter. Do I think the ladies will duel at dawn before that? *Non*. Do I think they'll try to score brownie points with the big guy and leverage their way to the top to de-throne Madame Dumont. *Absolument*."

I grinned. "The church ladies? That's ridiculous. They're a bunch of goody-two-shoes. Plus, you do realize you're talking about your own aunt, don't you? She has the ten commandments on a laminated card she carries in her purse. I know. She showed me the card."

"*Ma tante* is very good at catching flies with honey. Why do you think she's got *you* playing Bunny?"

"I'm confused. Am I the brownie she gets points with or the honey she gets flies with?"

Camille laughed. "Does it matter? Either way you're involved now. Me, I steer clear of *ma tante* and her church business. And I tried to keep you clear, too, but you blew it. If only you'd been in the car instead of off with Laurent I could have saved you."

Her remark reminded me of Claudette and Laurent's aunt-nephew moment. "Yeah, speaking of Laurent. What was with Claudette and all her finger wagging at him?"

"What finger wagging? I didn't see a finger wag." A barely contained smile came to Camille's lips. "So my big brother is in trouble, *hein*? It must be something good to distract *ma tante* from her church group." She pulled her phone from her purse. "*Une minute*. I'll find out." Before she put finger to screen, her phone buzzed with incoming text. She checked the message, tossed her mobile back in her bag, and motioned to the waiter for our bill.

"*Alors,* Laurent will have to wait," she said, waving her arm at me then collecting her jacket from the back of her chair. "*Allez.* Get your things. You're late already. We have to go."

I scurried to catch up with her sprint to the exit. "I'm late? I'm late for what? It's almost eight. I told Adam I'd be home early. The only plans I have for the rest of the night involve a bath and a book."

Adam was the guy I lived with and the precipitating factor in my move to a city that largely operated in a language I had yet to learn enough of to keep me out of accidental mishaps like agreeing to help with Easter pageants.

"*Had,*" Camille corrected me when we got to where she'd parked her car. "The only plans you *had* for the evening. *Maintenant* your date with the bath is off. Now, you have a new date. With the Easter Bunny."

3

"GEE, THE EASTER Bunny is older than I expected," I said to Camille. "And a lot less hairy. If you ask me, that guy looks more like Robert Redford's brother," I said.

"*Qui?*"

"Robert Redford. You know? The actor?"

"Right ballpark. Wrong actor. This one's a Québec actor and he's no Easter Bunny. But with this crowd he may as well be."

I glanced at the rest of the folks populating the giant room set off by strips of halogen lights bouncing off linoleum floors and walls slapped with grey paint. The bulk of the room held card tables with rickety chairs. At the tables, people of indeterminate age somewhere over sixty sat hunched over large sheets of paper, fat, bright highlighters in hand. Along a side wall, longer tables held large coffee urns, water jugs, and plates of various cookies and doughnuts. The farthest wall was fronted by a short stage. And the remaining side wall was dominated by clusters of onlookers milling about, heads facing the stage where Robert Redford's "brother" was talking into a microphone.

To the man's left sat a giant see-through globe bubbling with balls. To his right, a fake tree with dangling colored eggs hanging from branches of limp leaves. Behind him a string of lights, interspersed with more eggs, blinked with tiny bulbs twinkling like fireflies on a dark night. And flanking the edges of the stage, several woman hovered like eager fans waiting at a stage door.

Camille cocked her head side to side, taking in the Robert Redford lookalike as though weighing the possibility the two men were related.

"What is this place?" I asked Camille.

We'd come in the side entrance of a slim, two-storey building with no signage. Like a mini strip mall minus the glass fronts. With minimal windows and even less curb appeal. Whatever sign may have been on the front of the building went by in a blur before Camille zipped her car into the rear parking lot.

"It's an old department store," Camille told me. "It was driven out of business by online retailers. With the brick and mortar market drying up, the landlord decided to gut the place and now rents out the space for group gatherings, mostly to the church. This," she swept an arm in the air, "is tonight's *Les Femmes de l'Église* fundraiser bingo."

"Tonight's?"

"*Oui*. This set of bingos runs weekly throughout Lent. The project of Madame Jaffronelli."

"Ah" I said. "The first in line to the *Femmes* throne, right? Her plea for brownie points?"

Camille nodded just as my phone bleeped from my jacket pocket, and I checked the caller ID. My boyfriend Adam.

From a few feet away from where Camille and I stood, a woman sitting on a metal chair paused her knitting and clucked her tongue at me. She jabbed a knitting needle towards a French sign on the small table beside her. The sign practically eclipsed by a cash box and a coffee cup the size of a jumbo pop drink from a bodega back home.

Camille threw the woman a look and a short burst of French words.

The woman pointed to another sign posted on the wall behind her.

Camille groaned but pulled out her wallet, dropped some money on the table, then ignored the bingo sheets knitter lady slid at her by needle tip.

"*Heille là*," Camille said to me. "No phones at bingo. Better you leave the call or take it outside."

I glanced over at the Redford lookalike presiding over the stage, and I watched as the see-through globe circulating bingo balls spit out a ball, and "Redford" made a big show of calling out the number in first French and then English. He marked the number on a big white board behind him before turning his attention back to the spitting globe, pausing when someone yelled bingo and several older women from the wings closed in on him, a couple of the women with elbows raised.

I edged towards the "*Sortie*" sign to exit, torn between taking Adam's call and watching the elbows in action.

"Hey," I said into the phone when I got outside.

"Hey yourself," Adam said. "I thought you were coming home after dinner with Camille. Where are you?"

"Bingo."

"Excuse me? Did I hear you right? Did you just say you're playing bingo?"

A group of octogenarian men tumbled out the door behind me, half laughing, half grumbling, and I plugged my finger in my left ear to hear Adam better.

"I'm at Camille's aunt's bingo night run by the church ladies," I told him. "It's a long story."

"Do I want to hear this story?"

I laughed and one of the men turned my way and grinned. A wiry man across from him dabbed his forehead with a hankie and peeled a wad of tickets off a stack, sporting event tickets it looked like. He slowly handed the tickets to the first man who fanned the wad in my direction, his salt and pepper eyebrows attempting a synchronized wave move like two sections of spectators rising and falling in their seats at a concert. Only this guy's eyebrows couldn't seem to decide which section's turn it was to rise and which to fall.

I tried to keep my face from showing amusement lest the man think I was engaging him, and I let my eyes trail away.

"Lora?" Adam said.

"Yup. Still here. Sorry, it's a bit noisy. I'll catch you up when I get home, okay?"

"Sure. I'll be waiting with baited breath. And ice cream. Although if you want to get in on the ice cream you may want to hurry. I think the cat saw me bring it home."

We disconnected, and I pocketed my phone and smiled. I was a very lucky gal. I had ice cream waiting for me at home and a boyfriend who would think to get it for me. And two warm and furry critters, the aforementioned cat and also a dog, who probably also wanted in on the ice cream.

I went back into the hall to find Camille and tell her about said ice cream and entourage waiting for me. I found her by the stage, wedged between her aunt Claudette and church group ringleader Madame Dumont. Madame Dumont was dolled up exactly the same as when I'd last seen her, sooty eyebrows and all. Claudette had ditched the housedress she wore earlier for a pale blue pantsuit, her face now had enough makeup to get her a job at a department store cosmetic counter, and the bun in her hair was tidied into a chic chignon.

"What's going on?" I asked Camille.

"*Rien*. Slight disagreement about who sits next to Monsieur Ménard at the reception after bingo."

"Monsieur Ménard?"

Camille had one arm bracing each woman, so she tipped her head towards the Redford lookalike.

Automatically, I checked his wedding finger. No ring.

Madame Dumont's finger was not similarly bare, but that didn't necessarily mean anything. Claudette was a widow of some years and she still wore her wedding ring. Some widows seemed to do that. Even when Claudette had shown her first interest in dating recently, she'd still donned her ring. Like it had become part of her, an appendage that she'd no sooner consider ridding herself of as a foot.

A sixty-something woman approached Ménard and offered him a candy from a box in her hand. He accepted and she poured something into his palm. A butterscotch by the looks of it. He slipped it in his mouth and smiled at the woman as though she'd given him the biggest treat of his life. Which would be quite a coup since his life so far was probably closing in on eighty years.

Even without my social work skills or PI training, it was easy to see there was more going on at this bingo than fundraising.

"Who is that guy?" I asked Camille. "You said he was an actor? He must be really popular."

Camille nodded. "He was. About a hundred years ago."

Madame Dumont and Claudette both sucked in air.

"*Okay là*, okay. Maybe not a hundred years," Camille corrected.

I leaned in and whispered, "Is he single?"

"Single's got nothing to do with it," Camille said. "It's lineage."

I slid a look at Monsieur Ménard. His looks were Mediterranean, but tough to tell if he owed them to genetics or cosmetics. Either way I was sure the former was augmented by the latter given his age. Possibly a self-tanner and a box of hair dye.

But if I had to guess, I'd think there was some European heritage at play. Apparently, something that would set the church ladies a-titter.

"What? Is he related to some Pope or something?" I asked.

Claudette and Madame Dumont both sucked in air again and crossed themselves. Automatically. Like a salute.

"Or something," Camille said and pointed in answer to my question.

I tracked her point to a framed poster on the wall with a huge signature under the face of a young man with super short hair and a super wide grin. And a twinkle in his eye that for most of us would take special effects to create. Like a shimmering glint. Or maybe a rock star happy.

"Who's that?" I asked.

Camille leaned in closer. "That's Guillaume Ménard, the grandson of Monsieur Ménard. He's like the Québecois Ryan Gosling from his Notebook movie days."

I tried not to let my eyes trail to Claudette and Madame Dumont. They weren't exactly teenagers, but who was I to judge who caught their eye? We were long past the time of ageism when women couldn't show crushes on younger men.

A cackle of a laugh drew my focus back to Monsieur Ménard and his butterscotch lady friend. The cackle had come from Butterscotch who was batting her double set of false eyelashes at Ménard.

"*Et elle*," Camille said. "*C'est* Madame Jaffronelli. The first in line for the head of *Les Femmes de l'Église* group and the organizer of the bingos. It's her who got Ménard senior to guest host tonight to boost attendance."

Butterscotch lady aka Madame Jaffronelli looked vaguely familiar. Probably one of the women who'd had me surrounded in Claudette's foyer. The sweater and skirt outfit she wore didn't twig my memory, but her white blonde, shoulder length bob with the bow barrette on one side definitely did.

"Well, the Ménard men sure seem popular," I said.

Camille nodded. "They're also the stars of the film I told you about." She lowered her voice. "They're both playing the lead at different stages of life."

Ah, so maybe prestige and fifteen minutes of fame weren't the only things drawing the women to the throne. Maybe it had more to do with whom they'd be sharing that fifteen minutes of fame. Probably the lure of being immortalized in film alongside the Ménard men was no small deal to the ladies.

A ring came from the direction of Camille's pocket, and she excused herself to take her call outside. While she was gone, another elbow match broke out among the ladies, this one accompanied by lots of finger pointing and excited words, and refereed by a short man in a shiny grey suit.

A crowd of onlookers had abandoned their bingo tables and watched, their faces animated. I spotted the men I'd seen outside earlier, huddled together, alternatively giggling and cheering when the referee momentarily got caught in the women's fray.

"What's up?" Camille asked when she got back.

"Beats me," I told her. "But if they really want to raise charity funds, they could cordon off the stage like a boxing ring and sell tickets for the elbow matches. They're quite a show here. If one of the ladies doesn't end up with a black eye by the end of the night it will be a miracle."

Camille grinned as the church ladies' voices rose in a cacophony I'd bet had the suited referee longing for a whistle.

"Sounds like they're short money," Camille said. "Madame Dumont thinks Madame Jaffronelli counted wrong and *ma tante* thinks Madame Dumont didn't log things right because she was paying too much attention to Monsieur Ménard."

"And Madame Jaffronelli?" I asked.

"She thinks both the other ladies are nuts," Camille said. "She thinks someone is pinching money to make her look bad so her fundraising efforts will fall flat."

My eyes darted to the knitter guarding the cash box. Hard to imagine anyone pinching anything from her without having their fingers knitted into a knot.

"Is that even possible?"

Camille shrugged. "It sounds like it happens at every bingo. *Probablement* they're all nuts and their profits have gone up in doughnuts."

She eyed the refreshment table under attack from some of the bingo players who had abandoned their cards and shifted into after-game reception mode, filling little paper plates with goodies. Some of which, I noticed, were courtesy of a new addition, a tiered stand filled with brownies, making me think someone was taking the brownie points score thing literally. Also making me think Camille was right about me giving up chocolate for Lent. Brownies were my Kryptonite of baked goods. I'd only been off chocolate for a few hours and already I felt myself weakening.

The guy in the suit finally broke through the cacophony and began whisper-lecturing the ladies. Then the group disbanded. All three women stomping off in different directions.

"*Désolée, ma tante,*" Camille said, walking over to the refreshment table where her aunt had wandered and stood collecting abandoned paper plates. Camille bent and skimmed her aunt's cheeks with kisses. "I got a call and we have to go."

I lagged behind, just in case Claudette had a similar relationship to paper plates as Camille had to the slinky she kept on her desk at the office, and a paper plate suddenly found itself zipping through the air. I saw an entry point when Claudette's hands were empty and ventured in for my own goodbyes.

Claudette hugged me, pulling me close, and murmured in my ear. "Be a good girl, eh, *ma belle*, and go to make sure the costume fits."

"Costume?"

She eased away and her eyes narrowed towards mine. "The costume for you. For the egg hunt, of course."

Oh right. I'd nearly forgotten why we'd been summoned in the first place. Something to do with the Easter egg hunt. Something that apparently included a costume fitting.

"Um, what kind of costume is it?"

Claudette looked at me like I had two cards missing from my deck. "The Bunny, of course. It's you the Easter Bunny for the kids, no?"

Ah, so when Camille said I had a date with the Easter Bunny she'd meant my costume. Probably another detail lost on me in translation that I'd agreed to in my whiplash haze in Claudette's foyer.

Claudette jangled the keys on my new green bracelet. "This big one gets you in the side door of the church and this little one is for the padlock on the closet with your costume. Downstairs, just before the *petite cuisine*." Her eyes went to the cluster of women who'd migrated back to Monsieur Ménard. "And maybe take the suit home with you. Just in case."

"In case what?"

I felt her shoulder shrug against mine as she kept her eyes peeled on Monsieur Ménard's groupies. "In case nothing."

I nodded, sensing there was a whole lot of something in Claudette's nothing. Like maybe she thought somebody would sabotage her brownie points efforts by pinching the suit.

"Sure, okay," I told her. "I'll go first thing tomorrow."

She patted my arm, her gaze never leaving the church ladies.

"Tonight, *ma belle*. Tonight is better." And she gave my cheeks a kiss goodbye before venturing off to join the groupies.

4

I'D BEEN HOME less than five minutes when Adam came in from walking the dog, and they both trotted upstairs and into the bedroom where I perched on the edge of the bed taking off my socks.

Adam and I lived together in an old house he'd inherited from his mother. It had taken a while for us to migrate to the master bedroom and replace his mom's antiques with our own furniture. Even longer for the room to feel like ours, and there were still days I wasn't quite sure it did. But if anything helped in that department, it was the white metal bed I'd bought and topped with a plush mattress and billowy quilt. The bed's soothing comfort, a haven of sorts, particularly beckoned to me when I felt in need of a little solace. Like I did after my pop by the church closet.

Pong rushed over to my haven and presented her head for a pat as Adam closed the door and started towards me.

Stopping short, Adam let out a garbled noise and brushed at his shoulder. "What the—" He turned to the fluffy tentacle grazing his body and did a double-take. "What the heck is that?"

I let out a sigh and slumped onto the bed. "That," I said, "is my penance."

He lifted a hairy limb from the bundle of fluff hooked to the back of the door and took a closer look. "I'm gonna need more."

I sighed deeper and waved an arm in the air towards the ceiling from my flat-on-my back position on the bed. "I got a late start for Lent." I let my hand drop down to my side. "So when the church ladies said they needed a last-minute fill-in to help with the Sunday school kids' Easter festivities, I told them I'd be happy to help."

"Naturally," Adam said. "You helping out with kids makes perfect sense. All but the Lent and guilt part. You're not Catholic."

I turned on my side and rested my head in the crook of my arm to get a better look at Adam, his lanky body looking very basket-ball player in his slim jeans and sweatshirt. "Yeah, you'd think that would matter, but it doesn't. And fyi, that big lunch we had planned Friday at the Chinese food buffet to kick off our long holiday weekend of rambling walks and binging movies in bed is out. Apparently, we're fasting."

No need to tell him quite yet we'd also be ditching the choco-late splurge we'd been planning. A man could only take so much bad news at a time.

He shifted my legs and sat in their vacated place. "We?"

"Well you don't expect me to fast alone, do you? How long will I last if I have to watch you scarf down pancakes smothered in maple syrup and blueberries for breakfast? It's bad enough I have to wear that thing in public."

I pointed at the furry beast on the bedroom door. I was happy Claudette included me in such an important event and even a little jazzed when I understood I'd be playing Easter Bunny. Until I'd seen the costume. I'd imagined a cute bodysuit along with fake buck teeth and fun whiskers. Not a furry beast. I was going to look like Cousin It from the Addams' Family with big, pointy ears in that thing.

Adam ran a hand up and down my arm at a soothing pace. "Maybe it's not so bad. Maybe it just looks bad all limp like that on the hook. What's it supposed to be?"

I slipped onto my back and stared at the ceiling again. Anything not to look at the yellow and grey polyester get-up. "The Easter Bunny."

"Aw, well, see, that's kinda cute. The kids will love it. And you like dressing up. Remember the Halloween party where you dressed up like a cat? You looked awesome in that sleek tail and black bathing suit." He moved his mouth to replace his fingers on my arm and trailed a few kisses from my wrist to my elbow.

I rolled my eyes. "It was a leotard *not* a bathing suit. And I got to wear tights and do cat-eye makeup. That costume was nothing like this Bunny one. This one looks like someone stitched it together from an old carpet."

He looked at me and laughed. "You're exaggerating." He went to the door and unhooked the suit. "Try it on and you'll see. It's really not that bad."

Not that I believed him, but he was right about one thing: that I'd have to try it on sometime and that time may as well be now.

"Okay." I stood. "But it's going on over clothes. I'm not having that thing next to my skin. It smells like rancid furniture polish."

I ditched my clothes, dressed in old leggings and a cotton shirt, wiggled into the costume, and struggled with the zipper up my back, nearly toppling over with the effort of managing the Bunny head as I contorted to reach the zipper, finally giving up and letting Adam wrangle it into place. I took a moment to adjust the leg seams so the fanny didn't hitch up, and I plodded over to the mirror on the closet door.

My breath caught. At the sight or the smell, I wasn't sure. Maybe both.

In my reflection, a Bunny ear drooped and I propped it up only to have it deflate again when I let go.

My cat Ping wandered in from the hall, sniffed my leg, and ran under the bed.

"Ice cream," I said to Adam. "Stat."

He opened his mouth to speak, caught my eye, sealed his lip instead, and left the room.

"And don't even bother with a bowl," I called after him as he headed down to the kitchen. "Just bring the carton and a spoon. A soup spoon."

"WHO COULD POSSIBLY BE RINGING the doorbell in the wee hours of the morning?" I croaked to Adam, my mouth still dry from sleep, my eyes barely opening to slits.

I probed Adam's side of the bed when he didn't reply. Empty and barely warm.

The doorbell went again and Pong barked from her dog bed in the corner. I forced one eye open wider and peered at the clock. Five after eight. So, not so wee of an hour after all.

I pushed up from bed, rammed my feet into slippers, and shuffled downstairs.

"Claudette!" I exclaimed, answering the door to find Camille's aunt on my welcome mat.

"*Bonjour*," she said. Then taking in my nightgown and likely a frightful case of bedhead, her eyebrows creased and she leaned towards me. "You not well?" Her arm shot out as she spoke and her hand checked my forehead for fever.

"I'm fine," I assured her. I tugged my nightgown hem to my knees and invited her to come in, which she did, marching straight through to the hall, stepping out of her shoes en route before entering the inner house. She glanced from the living room doorway on her left to the staircase banking the wall on her right, then she continued her march forward to the kitchen at the back of the house.

The nearly century-old home Adam had inherited wore its vintage well. Classic solid features meets modern touches. Like the perfect vintage dress updated with Jimmy Choos and a Chanel bag. Which in kitchen house-speak translated to original wood cabinets updated with new counters and dusty-blue paint. And a row of windows adorned with airy café curtains overlooking the backyard.

As Claudette scanned the room, I snatched a note Adam had left on the fridge letting me know he'd already taken care of the pets morning needs and gone to an early meeting. Claudette paused her scan at the archway to the adjoining dining room and ventured over to sit at the pine round table set in the kitchen corner, her calf-length thin coat stretching at the buttons and her handbag resting on her lap.

I reached for a shirt Adam kept on the hooks by the sunroom door off the rear of the kitchen, and I offered Claudette some tea while I fashioned the shirt around me like a robe.

"Laurent waits for me," Claudette said, shaking her head to the tea invite. "I come only to see you got the suit."

I removed the kettle I'd started on the stove. "Laurent waits for you?"

She nodded. "*Dehors.*" She pointed to the front of the house. "Outside."

My eyes trailed to the main entrance, half-expecting to see Laurent in the doorway. "What's he doing outside?"

She shifted her bag. "I never come to your house before so Laurent bring me, and now he wait while I check the suit."

I eyeballed the front door again, wondering why Laurent hadn't come in with her. Double-parked maybe? Circling the block looking for a spot? On a business call? Or maybe it had something to do with Claudette's finger wag. Penance or something that had him playing her chauffeur for the morning.

Which got me wondering all over again what he had done to deserve the finger wag and how I could find out without appearing too nosey. Maybe curiosity really was a deadly sin. At least when it came to other people's personal business the rest of us had no business knowing about. Maybe curiosity is what I should have given up for Lent.

"You got it last night, eh?" Claudette said. "*Le costume?*"

The costume. Right. "Absolutely," I told her. I hadn't dared *not* get the outfit. Lest Camille's young cousins be right about Claudette and the Holy Ghost thing. Ditto now when Claudette wanted to see the shag-carpet Bunny. I fetched it pronto.

Claudette stood in the kitchen, her purse standing upright on the table beside her, when I got back with the suit. I draped the Bunny on a chair and stepped back.

Claudette smiled at me. "It's cute, no?"

I nodded. Sure, resting on the chair like that it looked a bit like a shaggy paper-doll Bunny.

She lifted it and held it up to me. "It fits okay?"

"Yup. Tried it last night and it fit fine."

She moved it closer to me, her fingers holding it taut shoulder-to-shoulder. She made a clicking sound with her tongue and shook her head.

"*Essaie-le*, okay? You try it so I can see."

I held in a groan at the idea of wrestling into the suit, and I stole a look at the clock on the stove. "Umm. I'm kind of late for work already. Maybe we could do that later. Really, it fits just fine."

Claudette's mouth pinched and her eye twitched.

"Or, you know what? Cancel that," I said with an inward sigh, reaching for the hanger. "Laurent knows you're here. I'm sure he won't mind if I take a few minutes."

I folded the suit over my arm and grabbed a jar from the counter and set it on the table where Claudette had been sitting.

"Please," I said. "Have something to eat and I'll just be a few minutes." I added a glass of water and a plate to the arrangement and pulled two muffins from the jar. I nabbed a muffin for myself and turned to go upstairs.

"*C'est quoi ça?*" Claudette asked as I neared the doorway.

"Excuse me?"

Claudette pointed at the muffin in my hand. "*Ça*," she said. "What's that?"

"Um. A muffin." A hint of embarrassment hit me. I'd made the muffins myself and truth be told their mushroom tops had overgrown some and misshapen into blobs.

She jabbed her finger closer to the muffin, poking at a fudgy mound. "*Non*. That."

With her thick French accent, her second word came out more "dat" than "that" but realization seized me instantly. I knew where she was going from the flash in her eyes, which may as well have been tiny crosses glinting.

My lips formed a sheepish grin. "Oops. Right." I set the muffin on the table. The muffin full of hunks of chocolate, my Lent no-no. "Almost forgot. No chocolate for me. Thanks for the reminder. This whole Lent thing is new for me." I made a show of swapping the muffin for a yoghurt and inwardly rolled my eyes at myself. Camille was right, choosing chocolate for my Lent offering was not my best idea. Avoiding chocolate was way harder than I predicted.

Claudette's eyes softened and she nodded. A good cue for me to dash upstairs. Better to face the carpet Bunny than a Lent lecture from *tante* Claudette. How she kept track of all the offerings on her mantel was a mystery to me, never mind that she noticed and remembered mine. Maybe she really did have magical powers. If so, I definitely wanted to keep on her good side.

When I got back to the kitchen in costume, half a muffin was gone and Claudette had the glass of water in her hand.

"Where's the feet?" she said, water sloshing side-to-side in her cup as she gestured towards the floor near me.

I looked down the grey carpet fur to my socks. "I dunno. This was all we found in the closet. We didn't see any Bunny feet." The "we" being me and Camille, who went into the church with me to retrieve the get-up. Turned out, the church was just down the street from the bingo place, and it had been an in-and-out mission, both of us eager to get on with our nights, and we could easily have missed seeing the feet.

Claudette shot out of her chair, moved the remaining muffin to the fridge, and rinsed her cup and jammed it in the dishwasher.

"*Allez*," she said, pushing me down the little hall to the vestibule.

"*Allez*?" I said. "*Allez* where?" I knew *allez* meant to go. Where the heck did she want to go? I stopped short when she whizzed around me and pried open the front door. "Whoa. I'm not going anywhere dressed like this. Just give me a sec to change." It was bad enough to think I'd have to be seen in the get-up on Easter by a bunch of kids and their parents. No way was I going to parade around the city in it on a regular weekday.

"It's fine," Claudette said, waving at me to catch up, widening the door, revealing Laurent standing on the porch.

Laurent's eyes locked with mine before he looked quickly away.

Oy. This Bunny suit was even worse than I thought. Laurent couldn't even look at it. So awful he didn't even tease me about it. What had I gotten myself into?

I retreated to the stairs. I was beginning to suspect Claudette's "*allez*" involved going back to the church in search of the Bunny feet, and I didn't even want to think about how much giant rabbit toes would up the ridiculous factor on this outfit. "Seriously. I'll just be a minute," I told her.

I zipped upstairs, not wasting any time. The minute thing was a big fib. I needed more than a minute. I didn't just need fresh clothes. I needed to wash my face and brush my teeth and swipe on lip gloss if I was going to face a day that included another visit to the church closet. And *excluded* chocolate.

5

---

*T*HEY WERE THERE all right. The Bunny feet. Far in the church closet corner. A set of shaggy grey paws. More yeti than rabbit. Poking out from below a swath of canvas hanging above. And intermittently lit by the lone light bulb I pulled on by its dangling string that swung like a pendulum and cast eerie shadows to and fro amid clouds of must, dust, and cleaner fumes.

I'd volunteered to run in and fetch the feet while Laurent and Claudette waited in the car, and now I was regretting it. The closet, as it were, was small and narrow. Hollowed out space between two rooms on either side that someone had slapped a door on to create a hideaway for storage. But that someone hadn't bothered to seal off the various pipes inside that wove in and out of the walls, floor, and ceiling and subdivided the closet into tiny modules at the corners that even young children would find a tight squeeze. It had been one thing the night before to get the costume which had been hanging center stage. It was a total other thing to have to crawl into the closet depths to retrieve the feet.

I sighed, shifted sideways, and shimmied in, making my way to the narrowed end, past old brooms and mops and pails, sucking in both my stomach and my breath because this bit of the cubby was apparently where everything went to die.

When I reached the end, I crouched and gingerly lifted the feet out of their hiding place, cringing at the scraggly uneven toenails, like chopsticks chiseled into pointy sticks, and the crunchy feel of the carpet-curl fur in my fingertips. The cheap polyester had an unexpected heft and felt like it had been wet and dried crusty countless times. An "ew" bubbled up in my throat despite my attempt to ward off notions about what accounted for the crusty texture.

At the sound of footsteps in the hall, I sent the "ew" on retreat, not wanting to be overheard squealing like a little girl. It was a good guess the footsteps belonged to Laurent, probably coming in to see what was taking me so long, and he was the last person I wanted to overhear me sounding squeamish. Off the clock, as Camille's brother and someone I worked with, I liked to think Laurent and I had become friends. But on the clock he was my boss, the vigilant kind, assessing my progress up the PI trail. And I was never quite sure when we were on the clock and when we were off.

I took a quick air exchange, holding on the inhale, and braced myself to back out all confident and competent, successful in my task of paw retrieval, when the closet light went out and a "slam" cracked in my ears. The unmistakable slam of a door shutting.

I scrambled backwards as best I could in the dark, making my way over to the crack of light near the floor, feeling my way up to the doorknob and rattling it. It moved but didn't release the door.

"Hey!" I called out. "Person in here!"

The echo of dulling footsteps was my only reply, so I called out again, louder. This time the footsteps paused then started up again at a brisker pace.

"Okay, fine," I said, nearly chocking on the furniture polish odors becoming concentrated and thicker by the second. "You've had your fun, whoever you are. Ha ha. Now open up."

Nothing.

Tiny tingles crept up my spine as the footsteps faded away. Whoever was out there had to have heard me. And it wasn't Laurent. Laurent wasn't the "lock-you-in-a-closet-for-fun" sort of guy.

Which meant whoever had shut the closet door on me just walked away leaving me locked inside. And wanted it that way.

"OKAY," **I TOLD** myself. *"Don't panic."* I grabbed for the plastic bracelet on my wrist and fingered the key for the closet. *"See. You have the key. It's all good."* I moved my hand towards the keyhole, fumbling around, gliding my fingers over the space below the doorknob. The space I found to be completely smooth. No hollow bits. No keyhole.

Right. Of course, because the key was for a padlock. And the padlock was on the other side of the closet door.

Okay, so maybe I could panic a little.

I banged on the door. "Hello! Hello! Anyone out there?!"

There had to be someone out there somewhere besides my unfriendly doorman, right? It was a church. And a Catholic one at that. Didn't people come in and out for masses? Didn't priests have to be on duty to hear confessions?

"Hellooo!"

I checked my pockets for my phone and came up empty. In all the rush leaving my house, I'd tossed the phone into my purse. The purse still sitting in Laurent's car while I made the quick dash into the church.

I blew out a puff of air and shifted away from something jabbing me in the side, nearly scalding myself on a pipe, forcing me to shift again and bang into something else. If I was stuck in here much longer, I'd be black and blue.

Remembering the closet had a light, I felt above me for the pull string and yanked it on, covering my nose with my other hand to limit ambient cleaner fumes from pushing their way in. The lighting didn't help much. It was dim, maybe 25 watts from an old bulb, frosted or clouded in dust. Which from what I could make out of the closet contents was probably a good thing. Not much I'd want to see. And nothing stood out as a possible help for getting me out.

I tapped the door and called out again. This time hearing footsteps getting louder. Yay!

"I'm stuck in the closet," I said to whoever was coming along. "Could you please let me—"

My unfinished question got cut off by a splintering blow, the door shook then opened, and a rush of cooler air mingled with the stifling closet stench.

I stumbled out and felt a firm hand steady me.

"Boy, am I glad to see you," I said, blinking to clear my watery eyes and letting out a cough. I didn't have to see straight to know the owner of the steadying hand. I recognized the touch. Laurent.

"*Bon ben, mon petit lapin,*" he said. "What were you doing in there?"

I blinked again. That may be the most he'd said to me all day. On the car ride over, he'd all but ignored me. Probably too embarrassed to make conversation after seeing me in the Bunny suit.

"When I went in the closet to get the rabbit feet, someone locked me in," I explained. Another cough spluttered out as I shifted the Bunny toes I clenched in front of me to my side. The last thing either of us needed was a visual aid to remind him of me kitted out in the carpet Bunny costume.

A thwunk accompanied my next cough, and the Bunny paws lost a chunk of weight. I looked down to see my shifting of the paws had overturned them and something had fallen out. Something white that bounced off my foot and tumbled away.

A second later, more weight dropped from the Bunny feet, and the thwunk was followed by a crash of glass shattering on the hard tile floor.

The piercing sound quickened my pulse, and I felt Laurent's hands clasp me again. This time, to airlift me several feet down the hall before depositing me on ground clear from the broken glass clustered like jagged pebbles amid a stream of red wine.

From around the corner, Claudette appeared with Mesdames Dumont and Jaffronelli flanking her, striding forward like football players taking the field. Almost in unison, their eyes dipped to the floor and their pace slowed to a stop.

The women shared surreptitious glances, eyelids at half-mast.

Laurent picked up the white blob that landed near the wall after its jump off my foot, and all three women sucked in air.

I edged closer to Laurent for a better look at the blob. Close up, it morphed into a bundle of cloth tied together with a thin string that nearly disappeared into the white fabric darkened with a smudge where the twine pinched. Laurent broke the knot on the string and unwrapped the bundle, letting the cloth wind itself out to reveal a wad of cash.

The women sucked in air again, and for a minute I felt sure another elbow fight would break out. Until the troop of women did an about face and began hoofing away.

"*Arrête!*" Laurent said.

The line of women stopped.

Laurent held the money wad aloft. "Aren't you ladies forgetting something?"

ALL THREE WOMEN shook their heads for the umpteenth time.

And this time I joined them, making Laurent, sitting beside me, swivel his look my way and add in his own head shake.

"*Ben*, let's try this again. So none of you knows anything about this money." As he spoke, Laurent tapped a stack of bills placed in the center of the table where we sat in the church kitchen. The table was long, thin wood with rounded metal feet at each end, and the top sounded hollow under Laurent's tap. The stack of money sat alongside more piles arranged by denomination, all counted out. And all adding up to the exact amount short from the previous night's bingo.

Which, if it was a coincidence, was one the investigator in Laurent thought worth further examination. Given my closet confinement, the happenstance had me curious, too. But not as curious as why three ladies who'd broken into an elbow match over the missing money barely more than twelve hours earlier had since morphed into *The Three Mumketeers* over the matter.

"And the bottle of wine that broke?" Laurent said.

Again more head shakes from the women sitting across from us.

"And none of you shut Lora in the closet?"

This got wide eyes and rigorous head shakes from the ladies.

"*Là Laurent, ça suffit!*" Claudette spoke up, placing her forearms on the tabletop and pushing herself to standing. "This is a time waste."

"Well at least now we know where the missing bingo money

went," Madame Jaffronelli muttered, clasping her hands in her lap. "I was right, *somebody* stole it to ruin my fundraising."

At that, all three women barraged each other with loud French words that ricocheted around the table, lots of finger pointing thrown in, until Madame Dumont shot up from her chair and faced Claudette, nose to chin.

"Anyone could have taken it," Madame Dumont shouted. She let her eyes drift until they landed on me. "Even your nephew or his little *copine*, Claudette. After all, it's them who had the money. Not us."

I felt my mouth drop open. Seriously? She was going to pin this on us?

Madame Dumont zeroed her pinpoint eyes domed in sooty brows in on me. "And his *copine* was there last night when the money went missing. *Pis*, she has the key for the closet."

"Hey," I said. "You gave me that key. I never asked for a key."

Madame Jaffronelli clapped her hands together. "That's right," she said, glaring my way, her words perfect English with a touch of Italian undertone. "You did have a key. And you went to the closet last night."

Okay, I could see how that didn't sound so good. Still, that was no reason to assume I took the money. What would I want with their money?

"That's circumstantial evidence at best," I said and noticed a small smile come to Laurent's mouth.

Claudette glared at him and his smile faded.

Oh my. Was Claudette starting to doubt me, too?

"*What's everyone doing in here, hein?*"

I placed the voice even before Camille came into my peripheral vision as she strode into the room. She stopped at the head of the table and eyed the loot set atop like a centerpiece display.

Short French tsk sounds slipped from Camille's lips as she

turned, headed for the counter, and pulled a mug from a hook fastened on the underside of an upper cabinet. *"Franchement!* It's not nice to dip into the collection plate." She pulled a coffee pot from the stove and filled her cup, nearly gagging when she took a sip of her fill. "Aye!" She scrunched her nose. "Okay, I take it back. Dip into the collection plate and buy a proper coffee machine before you kill people with that swill!"

"This money's not from the collection plate," I told her. "It's from last night's bingo. At least we think it is. It seems to be the money that was missing."

"Oh," she said. "Then it's good you found it, *hein?*" Her gaze went from me to the church ladies. "But you could still use it to buy a coffee machine. That's what the bingo extras are for, no? To help the church and the needy? *Croyez-moi,* better coffee would do both."

Camille dumped the rest of her coffee down the sink, gave her cup a quick swipe and rinse, and placed it in the dish drainer. She turned to face the table, palming a slip of gold foil and crunching something in her mouth, thirty seconds or so passing before she spoke again. This time her words clearly directed at me. "You ready?"

"Ready for what?" I said.

"Voyons, Lora. Ready to go. *Ma tante* called to say you needed a ride to the *bureau."*

I glanced at Claudette wondering when she'd had the chance to call Camille. And whether or not her request to have me chauffeured away from the premises was about more than niceties. Since I'd come with Laurent, I could leave with him. Unless Claudette had other reasons for wanting me gone in a jiff. Like maybe she really did suspect me of having something to do with the missing money and wanted time alone with Laurent to report her misgivings.

No, that was absurd, right? She wouldn't fall for the ramblings of the other church ladies. Claudette trusted me. She wanted me to be the church Easter Bunny for goodness sake. She'd even insisted on the *tout de suite* Bunny feet pickup to be sure I had the whole costume in order.

"*Vraiment, ma tante?*" Laurent said. "You called Camille?"

Claudette kept her attention fixed on the empty chair she'd vacated, as though tucking it into the table took great concentration. When she finally raised her eyes, they went solely to Laurent.

"There's nothing more for Lora to do here, *n'est-ce pas, mon grand*? Or for us. You take me home and Lora can go to work with Camille. The rest is a matter for *Les Femmes de l'Église* to discuss later." She gave quick nods to Mesdames Dumont and Jaffronelli who exchanged looks then offered reluctant nods back.

Seemed to me the other two women were giving in a bit easily after their big show of accusing me, but if they were willing to let it go so was I. And so long as I was left out of it, Claudette was right, the whole thing was a church matter and didn't really concern any of the rest of us. I for one was happy to let them sort it out. The missing money turning up in a closet was odd and all, but it wasn't exactly the caper of the year or anything.

"*Parfait,*" Camille said, swinging her arm between me and the doorway. "Then we go."

With a glance back at Laurent, quiet and wearing his unreadable face, I joined Camille to leave. We were out to her Jetta and halfway to the office before I remembered about my purse left behind in Laurent's car.

6

"**WAIT, SOMEONE LOCKED** you in the church closet?" Camille said.

"Yup." I paused in the recounting of my morning so far, which I'd started with Claudette's visit to my house and ended with the money and wine tumbling out of the Bunny feet and the church ladies accusations about me.

We were in Camille's Jetta stopped at a red light, and her hand went to her handbag. Brushing her fingertips together, she veered away from the bag and grabbed onto the steering wheel again.

"Go ahead," I said. "It's fine."

The light changed and the car edged forward barely a car length then stopped again.

Camille craned her neck to see around the traffic. "Go ahead what?"

"Go ahead and take a chocolate. You know you want one."

"*Voyons*. I can't eat chocolate in front of you. You gave it up for Lent, remember?"

Remember? Of course I remembered. It was hard *not* to

remember. The mere thought of chocolate conjured the image of Claudette's glinting eyes like some flash from a horror movie. Since "the look" over the muffins at my house, I couldn't forget about the Lent chocolate deal I'd made if I tried.

"Really, it's fine," I assured her. "You ate chocolate after your coffee at the church and it didn't bother me at all."

This was a slight fib. I may have had a moment of longing when I spied the gold-foil chocolate skin that she'd palmed in her hand.

"That was different," Camille said. "That was emergency chocolate. Something to cleanse my palate from the horrible brown water in that coffee pot."

Her mouth and nose scrunched at the memory, and she edged the Jetta forward another car length. Apparently, traffic up ahead was entering the intersection on a one-at-a-time basis.

"Oh for goodness sakes," I said. I pulled Camille's purse from where she'd set it between us, reached inside, and grabbed a handful of wrapped chocolate balls. I unsheathed one and passed it to her. "Consider it more palette cleansing."

She accepted my offering and smiled. "Did I ever tell you you are my favorite friend ever?! And your will power is inspiring. Maybe next Easter I will give up something real for Lent in your honor."

"Chocolate?"

She grinned. "*Je t'ai dit* your will power is inspiring not lobotomizing."

"Is that even a word?" I said on a laugh.

She shrugged and sighed when the traffic light turned red again.

"Seriously, what would you give up?" I asked. "Coffee?"

"Make it that church coffee and it's a plan."

"Deal," I said. "And next year I'm giving up playing Easter Bunny for your aunt's church group. No offense, but those ladies are a bit crazy. I can't believe they'd think for one minute that I would steal their bingo money."

Camille took another chocolate. "Well, they did come along and find you with it."

"No. What they saw was me, and your brother I may add, finding a bundle wrapped in cloth that turned out to contain money. There's a difference."

The light went green and Camille got the car into gear again. "Still."

"Still what?" I said.

"Still, to them it may look suspicious."

"Seriously? That makes no sense. If I *had* taken their money why would I hide it in *their* church? Or be parading around with it? Why wouldn't I just have taken the money home with me?"

"*Peut-être* because I was with you after you stole it, and when we were getting the rabbit costume, you didn't want me to see the money so you stashed it in a foot."

"Right. And then left the foot, er Bunny paws, in the church closet? Just whose side are you on?"

"Yours. Of course yours. I'm just trying to see the other side."

"There *is* no other side!"

Camille's mobile trilled from somewhere deep in her purse.

"Get that, will you?" she said.

I dug in her bag for her phone, and she glanced at the screen.

"It's you calling," she said. "That's a neat trick."

"No trick," I told her. "I left my purse with my phone in Laurent's car."

"Open it on speaker," Camille said then called out, "*Allô?*"

"Am I on speaker?" Laurent's voice asked.

"*Bien oui,* you're on speaker. I'm driving," Camille told him.

"Tell Lora I have her phone and she has a message."

"Tell her yourself. You're on speaker!"

"What's the message?" I interjected.

Laurent paused a beat then said, "It's from Adam. He's with Tina at the hospital. She's in labor with the twins."

Tina was an old college friend of Adam's who dialed in and out of our lives and had more recently kept us dialed in after naming Adam godfather to her firstborn sons who were soon to be making their entrance into the world. Tina tended to broadcast at a frequency that grated a bit, and we weren't exactly friends ourselves, but for Adam's sake I was learning to keep her on auto-tune to smooth out her highs and lows.

"Labor?" Camille said. "Are you sure Adam said it was labor?"

Laurent confirmed the wording.

Camille drummed her fingers on the steering wheel. "I thought Tina planned a C-section for the babies."

I nodded. "She did. Next week. Something must have changed."

I asked Laurent for the hospital details, and Camille switched our destination route.

"Meet us there," Camille shouted into the phone when she veered for a last-minute turnoff. "And bring Lora's things. It's creepy getting calls from Lora when she's right here."

She jabbed her finger at the phone to end the call, and I dropped the phone back into her purse. Along with some choco-lates taken out earlier, my fingers holding onto one briefly hoping to absorb it by some kind of food osmosis.

Camille eyed me. "Go on, have some. It's dark. Very good. You could always say for Lent you meant only to give up milk choco-late not dark."

"Like *Mignon* and his flavored sticks?" I said, mulling over her suggestion.

"*Exactement.*"

"Isn't that kinda cheating? I mean it's okay for a dog to bend the rules since he's not really voluntarily participating, but it seems wrong for me to cheat."

"It's not cheating. It's being specific. It's being clear with your intentions."

"You mean like your intention to give up peanut butter even though you don't even like it?"

"There are lots of things we don't like that we still do, Lora. It still counts. Or, think of it another way. It's like being a good negotiator. Like when you're making a deal and ask for something you don't really need knowing the other party will take it off the table. When he does, it makes him feel like he got a win. But really you never wanted it in the first place so everyone is happy."

I eyed the chocolate again. Camille may have missed her calling as a lawyer. She was making a great case for eating the chocolate.

"No," I said, shuttling any errant chocolates into her purse and zipping it shut. "It's only a couple more days. I can do without chocolate for a few days. I didn't even like chocolate so much until I met you Carons."

"That's because you never had the *right* chocolate before you met us. Sometimes you don't know what's missing until you find it."

I sighed as Camille pulled the car into hospital parking. She was right of course. But if I told her so, she might re-open the subject and sway me over to the "dark" side, as it were, because truth be told my will power wasn't as strong as she thought. Especially when it came to the Caron sway. Nobody did temptation better than the Carons.

NATURALLY, TINA HAD a private room. Those could be hard to come by at the hospital, but somehow she'd snared one. Not a surprise. Private rooms often came with an added cost and her husband Jeffrey, being a lawyer and all, probably had good insurance to cover perks like that. But even if he hadn't, an hour with Tina probably had all the other moms-to-be wishing they'd opted for home births. And the nurses scrambling to find someplace to sequester Tina.

"I don't want *another* doctor," I heard Tina say, voice rising with each word, as I lingered outside her doorway. "I want *my* doctor."

"Your doctor is out of town for the long weekend," a young nurse explained. "But Doctor Schector is very good. She's delivered lots of twins. You're in expert hands."

"I don't *want* to be in expert hands, I want *my* doctor. Jeffrey, do something."

I moved a bit closer to peek deeper into the room. From my vantage point, I could see Tina's socked feet sticking out at the end of her bed and a nurse hovering not far off. Tina's husband Jeffrey stood midway up the bed, so I could only make out half of him. And half of Adam sitting in a vinyl armchair placed along the wall on the other side of the bed.

Adam had his arm bent as though his hands were intertwined like when he was just about to crack his knuckles. A habit that mainly showed itself when he was around sick people or hospitals. Something I'd learned when we'd first moved to Montreal and his mom was undergoing cancer treatment. Instantly, I felt bad for loitering in the hall and delaying my entry, my sense memory kicking in and impelling me to buttress him. Only in this case, I wasn't sure what he needed buttressing for since Tina sounded like her usual self, full of vim and vitriol.

"*Alors?* What are you doing out here?" Camille whispered, coming up beside me.

Camille had made a pit-stop by the washroom when we got out of the elevators. I suspected her stop-by had less to do with a visit to the little girls' room as it did with delaying her own visit to the big girl's room. Camille had aversions to both hospitals and Tina, so it was a wonder she'd come in with me at all.

"You'll just have to get my doctor back. That's all there is to it." Tina's voice floated out into the hallway. "I'll wait."

I didn't have to peek into the room again to know Tina probably had her arms folded over her maternity bra boobs as she spoke.

"Ah. *Je comprends*," Camille said. "Tina is having a moment. You're right. Better to wait out here." Her eyes trailed over to the bank of elevators. "Or maybe we should just go. It sounds like she's busy anyway."

A set of elevator doors opened and Laurent walked out. Followed by *tante* Claudette, who had a stuffed teddy bear tucked under one arm and a small gift bag in the other, her handbag dangling from her wrist.

Camille cheek kissed her aunt and relieved her of the gift bag, sliding the tissue paper top aside to peer inside. "What's this?"

"*Des cadeaux*. For the mom and baby," Claudette said.

"Babies," Camille corrected. "And you don't even know the mom and babies."

Claudette reached to take the bag back and spoke a stream of clipped words in French. Something to do with manners and etiquette I think. Something that got Camille looking at her own empty hands and tapping her foot.

"Okay," she said. She tugged me down the hall past the elevators. "Wait here a minute. I'll grab us something from the gift shop and be right back."

I wanted to tell Camille not to bother, that there was plenty of time for that later. That this visit was just to check in and make sure everything was all right with Tina's delivery given the date change. But I didn't say a word to stop Camille. I didn't want to give Claudette two reasons to question my character in one day.

Since she'd arrived, she'd avoided direct eye contact with me, weighing down my heart and making me think the earlier morning's events with the bingo money weren't completely behind us yet.

Camille disappeared into the next available elevator, leaving me alone with Laurent, who took advantage of the lull in activity to pass me my purse, and Claudette, who nudged him aside and curtly asked how I knew the mom-to-be.

I transferred my phone from purse to pocket and gave Claudette the short version of how Tina had come into my life, Claudette nodding along, giving me the impression the story was not new to her. Probably Laurent had filled her in on the ride over. He had to have said something to explain the detour in his chauffeuring duties. A detour, that by the look on his face, was not all that welcome. But then he barely knew Tina and had already lost a good part of his morning to the church closet chaos and probably wanted to get on with his day.

The nurse from Tina's room came into the hall and zipped past us so fast I felt her smock flutter against the back of my legs as she went by. Ordinarily, that kind of thing happening in a hospital would have me thinking words like "Code Blue" or something, but having been privy to snippets of the nurse's conversation with Tina, I figured the swift exodus had more to do with remedying Tina's doctor dilemma.

"I thought I heard voices out here," Adam said, popping into the hall and over to me, taking in our threesome. "Um. It's so nice of you all to come."

Claudette put on a smile and darted a look to Adam then to Laurent.

I watched as Laurent launched into introductions between Adam and Claudette, and I tried to remember if they'd ever met officially.

Adam went to shake Claudette's hand and got an extra shake from the teddy bear tucked under Claudette's arm.

"Adam is the godfather for the babies, *ma tante*," Laurent added to the introduction.

Claudette's face lit up. "The godfather, well, that's a big honor!" She threw a furtive glance my way. "To be godparents is a big responsibility."

"Only Adam is a godparent," I clarified. "The godmother is a relative of Tina's husband."

Claudette nodded understanding and something dimmed in her eyes. Probably irked somewhat by the division of godparent duties. Like it was some break in godparent protocol or something.

I didn't bother to tell her I thought the godparent mantle was more ornamental than practical in this case given I didn't think Tina or Jeffrey was particularly religious. Mostly, I thought Tina had named godparents because she thought it upped her social cachet or gave her a reason to have a fancy ceremony or haul in fancier baby gifts.

"How are things going with Tina?" I asked Adam. "How come she's here now and not next week?"

"Her water broke. Only her doctor didn't expect her to go into labor early so he's not here. They assigned her another doctor who says the babies are in good position with no distress and Tina's perfectly fine to have a, um, natural delivery and doesn't need a C-section like she'd planned. But Tina wants a second opinion."

"Wouldn't she rather deliver than have the C-section?"

Adam shook his head. "I think she had her heart set on the C-section."

I couldn't imagine anyone having her heart set on a surgery when it could be avoided. But then birthing two babies didn't sound so fun to me, either, so what did I know?

The nurse from Tina's room hurried past us again, this time going in the opposite direction and with a young doctor in tow. An intern maybe. The doctor had her hair in a long braid with bunched strands sticking out like bird wings trailing down her back, and she had crinkles around her eyes that belonged on someone over fifty.

"I better get back in there," Adam said, turning to go. 'That looks like the new doctor.'

"Isn't Jeffrey with Tina?" Laurent asked.

"Yeah," Adam said. "But he missed a bunch of the prenatal classes that I went to so Tina doesn't think he understands everything that's going to happen. She wants me there to help Jeffrey see her point of view once the doctor puts in her opinion."

"*Alors*, you're like the doula."

We all turned to Camille who had somehow managed to sidle up behind me unnoticed and spoken over my shoulder.

Adam shrugged. "I guess." He turned towards Tina's room, promising to be back with an update when he knew more.

Camille tapped her foot. "*Voyons*, how long is this going to take?" She shuffled over to a line of chairs under a window a ways down from the elevators and deposited two big gift bags tied with ribbons and bows onto a chair.

The rest of us joined Camille, and I asked her what was in the bags.

Camille waved a hand in the air. "I don't know. If it was cute and blue it went into the bags."

I smiled. Camille's version of speed shopping. Normally, she preferred to shop in boutiques. Get her into a chain store, or in this case, a hospital version of a chain store, and she bolted in and out so fast the security cameras probably logged her as a blur.

Claudette set herself on the edge of a chair, shifted the teddy bear to her lap, and checked her watch.

Laurent angled himself to look out a window, and I scanned various announcements posted on a wall.

Five minutes of scanning, foot tapping, and watch checking later, Adam ambled back into the hall and over to us.

"It looks like it will be a while before Tina delivers," he said. "You guys may want to come back later this afternoon."

Claudette immediately stood and brushed bits of teddy bear fluff from her dress. Camille collected her gift bags. And Laurent shifted his gaze to the elevators.

Maybe I had it wrong. Maybe it wasn't just Camille who hated hospitals. Maybe all Carons had an aversion for them. Admittedly I wasn't fond of hospitals, either, but it didn't seem right to leave Adam on his own. This was a big deal. Tina was the first in our immediate friend circle to start a family. And Adam wasn't just her friend, he was going to be godfather to her babies, so this was a big day for him, too. Which meant it was an important event in both our lives.

"Yes," I said. "Why don't you all go and I'll catch up with you later."

Camille and Claudette moved to the elevators and hit the down button.

Laurent held back, lingering by the window, reminding me of the smudgy line between us of boss/employee versus friends. It *was* a workday and I hadn't exactly asked for time off, after all.

Camille spotted her lingering brother, went to collect him, and got stuck in a *tête-à-tête* instead that got drowned out by the piercing screech of Adam's name filling the air.

I turned to see Jeffrey's head pop out from Tina's room as another screech let loose behind him. Jeffrey directed glazed eyes our way, arm swinging at Adam like he was waving a boat to dock.

"Looks like I gotta get back in there," Adam said to me. "It's okay, you go. This is going to get messy before long. Tina's telling everyone her husband is a lawyer and she'll sue if she doesn't get her C-section." He held me in a hug and dropped a kiss on my cheek. "Save yourself and come back later. I'm sure it will be hours yet before she has the babies either way."

Before I could respond, Adam released me and had already closed half the distance back to Jeffrey.

The elevator doors opened, and I shuffled in with the Carons, squeezing in next to Camille.

"So," I said to her. "You want to stop by somewhere for a late breakfast or grab a takeout brunch for the office?"

"We're not going to the office. We've got a new investigation to do. It seems after we left *Les Femmes de l'Église* this morning, Madame Dumont hired Laurent to investigate."

Uh oh. I skipped a look at Claudette in the corner of the elevator, still clutching her giant teddy bear, her mouth set, eyes on the ceiling.

Probably I knew where this was going, but in case I was mistaken I asked, "To investigate what?"

"You mean whom?"

I winced as the elevator kicked to life with a plunge that left my stomach several floors above. "Okay then, whom?"

"You."

7

"*T*HIS MAY BE the easiest case you ever had," I said. "Shut before it's even open. I had nothing to do with the bingo money."

After a quick stop for decent coffee and a couple bagels, Camille and I were back at the rent-a-space we'd been in the night before. Aka the scene of the crime.

Only now, instead of an old local celebrity and a bingo ball center stage, a harried forty-something woman in sensible shoes and a track suit scurried around the stage after a gaggle of young kids. The kids flitted about in partial costumes, the girls in tutus with wings made of veil fabric, and the boys dressed as woodsmen. They all dashed around skinny trees made of green paper leaves, then they circled a short, long table covered in a cloth the kids kept pulling off and flapping at each other. In rehearsals for the Easter pageant I was told. What tutus and woodsmen had to do with Easter was beyond me.

Every now and then, one of the flitting kids would flit over to the corner, toss money and strips of paper on knitting lady's table, and flit back to the stage before knitting lady even had the money tucked in her cash box. Each time, causing the woman in the track suit to frown and resume her wrangling.

"*Bien entendu*, you had nothing to do with the money," Camille said, swinging her attention from the kids to me. "Everyone knows that."

I thought of Claudette averting my eyes at the hospital, the sinking feeling resurfacing along with the memory. "You sure?"

"Of course I'm sure." Camille leaned down from her chair beside me and unzipped her knee-length boots. "*Mon Dieu, il fait chaud ici! Et j'ai tellement soif.*"

I nodded and unbuttoned my jacket. I didn't get all of what she said, but I understood the part about being hot and thirsty. The heat had to be cranked up to eighty degrees. I was starting to understand about the girls with the wings. The wings made like fans when the kids ran around. Probably it was all that was keeping the rest of us from fainting.

"What's up with the heat?" I said.

"The thermostat is probably stuck. It happens a lot."

"And nobody fixes it? That's crazy."

Camille removed her jacket and threw it on an empty chair down the row where we sat amid a makeshift collection of audience seating set in tiers facing the stage. "The janitor from the church tries, but it never helps. Now they just report it to the landlord, he gives them a break on the rent, and everyone's happy." Camille peeled off her sweater and aired the blouse underneath.

"Have a chocolate, Camille. You'll feel better," Laurent said, materializing on her other side, newly arrived from his detour to drop off Claudette.

"I can't eat chocolate in front of Lora. It's her Lent offering," Camille told him.

I sighed. "We've been through this. It's fine. You ate it twice already and I was fine. It's not a problem." I smiled. "It's not like me eating peanut butter in front of you. That would be wrong."

"Peanut butter?" Laurent said.

"Camille's Lent offering," I explained, sitting forward to better see him.

"Camille doesn't even like peanut butter," he said.

I threw a smile his way to include him in my joke. "Exactly what I said. But she said it still counts."

Laurent shook his head at his sister's logic.

"So what did you give up, big brother?" Camille asked, an indignant note in her voice. "Something huge and important I suppose."

Laurent stayed quiet.

"That silly, *hein?*" Camille said. "You won't even admit what it is. Go on, tell us. We won't judge."

Still Laurent said nothing.

Camille crossed her arms over her chest. "Fine. Be like that and keep it to yourself."

I waited a beat to let them settle their sibling squabble and was about to ask what our plan was now that we were all present and accounted for, when another woman came in through a door at the back and stood by the stage. This woman sixtysomething with a blonde bob, a giant brown bow cinching hair to one side of her head. Madame Jaffronelli. She slid a look at the harried woman busy with the kids, then she gestured at me to join her at the improvised backstage cordoned off by a curtain, her movement discrete, almost conspiratorial.

I tapped Camille, whispered to her that I'd been beckoned, and made my way to the curtained area. I created a slit in the fabric with my hand and slipped in to find racks of costumes and a chipped, floor-length, wood-framed mirror propped against a wall. And Madame Jaffronelli who clasped my forearm and drew her face close to mine.

"I want you to know I don't think you had anything to do with the missing money," she said, her words drifting out on a hint of butterscotch. "I can tell, you are a good girl."

"Um. Thank you," I said, my voice rising some by my last word and approaching questioning tone. "I appreciate your confidence."

She dabbed sweat from her upper lip with her sleeve. "It's all Madame Dumont. Don't take it personally, mind you. She's a suspicious type."

"Okay. Good to know."

Madame Jaffronelli cocked her head at me and went on. "Madame Dumont is just looking for someone to blame so she doesn't look bad. As the head of our group, the money is her responsibility. She wants a way to explain the missing funds to the priest, so she can hold onto her position in *Les Femmes de l'Église*."

"Right." Through a gap in the curtains, I spotted Laurent approaching the tiny ad-hoc backstage that Madame Jaffronelli had chosen for our little *tête-à-tête*.

Madame Jaffronelli must have heard him approach, too, because she released my arm and moved a hand to smooth her hair before she turned around and greeted him.

Bustling forward, she patted him on the arm. "I like very much your little *amie*," she told him, throwing a smile my way. "My Alexandro is holding the car for me, so I'm off now. I leave you with your friend."

"What was that all about?" Laurent asked me when Madame Jaffronelli was gone.

"I'm not sure," I told him. "Only that Madame Jaffronelli doesn't peg me as the thief. She seems to want me to know it's Madame Dumont flinging around accusations to protect her position in the church group."

"Interesting."

"Is it? Doesn't seem very interesting to me. The whole thing is ridiculous. Trying to bring me into their missing money battle is silly. Just because I was there when the money showed up. You were there, too. Why aren't you catching any flak?"

"Nobody is catching flak. You're catching attention."

"Excuse me?"

"It's like a magic act. Get the audience to look somewhere else while the magician pulls his trick."

"So you're saying I'm a distraction?"

His lips tightened. Containing a smile maybe. Or a grimace. "That's one way to put it."

"Hmm. Then you're also saying someone is acting like the magician."

"*Bon ben*, somebody took the money and put it in the closet."

"And that somebody doesn't want us focused on that."

"Right."

I toyed with the sleeve of a flannel shirt hanging on a rack, my focus on a loose thread. "And what about your aunt?" I said, my voice dropping. "Does *she* think I took the money?"

A beat passed then Laurent said, "*Ma tante* has to go along with her group's wishes."

My eyes strayed from the sleeve to Laurent's face. "That's not an answer."

He shrugged. "All I know is that Madame Dumont has bought the act and if we don't reveal the magician to her, she's going to report you for theft. She's given me 24 hours to prove your innocence or she goes to the police."

"That's crazy. This isn't even the first time money went missing. They can't possibly blame me for those other times, too. No cop would believe it."

"*Peut-être*," Laurent said. "But a report will still be filed for this theft and won't look so good for somebody in investigator training soon to be applying for a PI license."

I did a slow blink, trying to figure out how offering to help with some Easter festivities could have led to a threat to my career plans. It really was true. No good deed did go unpunished. "This is unbelievable. Even for a magic trick."

Laurent nodded. "*Oui*. Now let's go find the missing magician before you end up spending Easter at the PDQ."

8

"*I*S THIS REALLY necessary?" I asked.

"*Voyons*, Lora," Camille said. "The best way to prove you didn't take the money is to find out who did. Just get it over with already."

Easy for her to say. Nobody asked her to stuff herself into the stinky church closet and poke into its dark recesses. I wasn't buying this "return to the second scene of the crime" nonsense as a place to start our search. It wasn't even technically the scene of an actual crime. The discovery of evidence of a crime maybe. Probably Camille just wanted me otherwise occupied so she could scarf down chocolate out of my view.

"What makes you think there's more money stashed in the closet?"

"*Mais alors*, this isn't the first time the bingo was short money. If someone's been stealing it and storing it in the closet, probably they've been doing it for a while. It's possible all the money is in there."

I pinched my nose closed like a swimmer about to jump into

the deep end of a pool, and I dipped my head into the tiny closet front, looking left and right into the deepest sections on either side. Less than ten seconds later I was out. "The cupboard is crammed with stuff. Money could have been shoved anywhere. I won't last a minute in there."

Of course, I'd lasted longer than a minute when I'd been locked in the closet. But that was different. That was accidental. This was avoidable.

Camille rummaged in her purse, withdrew a tiny pouch, and passed it to me.

I held up the clear package to get a closer look. "Are those nose plugs?"

Camille nodded.

"What are you doing with nose plugs?"

"They're for the *centre sportif*. I don't like water up my nose."

Sure. Made sense. Camille belonged to a gym. As did Laurent. Both of their physiques so fit and toned they could be mistaken for athletes. And probably had the lung capacity of athletes, too.

I thrust the nose plugs at her. "You do it," I said. "You're better at holding your breath."

She shoved them back at me. "But you're better at crawling into small spaces."

I sighed. I was beginning to think my petite size was the only reason Camille and Laurent hired me at C&C. Not because I fit the job requirements but because I fit in small spaces.

"Fine," I said, taking the plugs from her. "I'll go in. But you better have gloves in that bag of yours, too, because I'm not touching anything that feels as cringe-worthy as the Bunny feet."

Ten minutes later I was done my search. No more money finds, but I did find more wine tucked into big coat pockets, buckets, and the like, along with a few other bottles of booze. All of it, I'd passed out to Camille who had the bottles collected on the floor, arranged like the two back rows of bowling pins, and she was snapping a picture of the lot with her phone camera.

I scanned her bottle display. "Somebody sure picked a bad spot as a wine cellar. It's like ninety degrees in there with the door shut."

Camille picked up one of the wine bottles. "*Oh là là*. I hope very much this is not the communion wine. It would take a miracle to make this stuff drinkable. This isn't wine at this point, it's poison."

"Well, if our money thief stashed it and he's been drinking it, that would make our job easier. All we'd have to do is check hospitals for any poison victims who showed up since bingo night."

"Why do you think it's the thief who stashed the wine?" she asked me.

"Both the wine and the bingo money fell from the Bunny feet. Even if they were each put in a different foot, it'd be pretty coincidental for each to have been placed by different people."

Camille looked back at the booze collection. "*Voyons*, if it is the same person who hid both, maybe he took the money to buy better wine. This stuff looks like it came in bulk at a big box store."

I didn't know much about wine, so I'd have to take Camille's word on that. One bottle had an appealing flower on the label, but probably that didn't speak so much to good quality as good marketing.

I scanned up from the bottles to the padlock hanging from the open closet door. "Even if the thief did, looking for a big box store shopper wouldn't narrow things much. But I'm guessing not a lot of people have a key to the closet. That should help us."

"*Oui et non*," Camille said. "All the women in *Les Femmes de l'Église* group have keys, and there's one kept with all the other church keys in the maintenance room. Theoretically, anyone could get their hands on a key with little effort. And it still wouldn't rule you out in the eyes of Madame Dumont."

Ugh. Right. Back to me again. "Okay so if access isn't the main issue, how about motive? I mean, maybe it's a Venn diagram thing. Put a list of names in the 'A' circle of people with immediate key access, you know, since there's no way of knowing who all may have had secondary key access. Next, put a list of people who would want to take the bingo money in the 'B' circle. Then we see if any names intersect in the subset 'C' circle."

Camille raised an eyebrow at me. "*Wanting* money is usually the motive to taking it. That doesn't exactly limit the 'B' circle pool.'

"True. But to take something that doesn't belong to you also takes different morals. Or more motivation. Like greed or revenge." Or thwarting your fellow group members chances of winning the upcoming election. But that motive I kept to myself.

Through the open closet door, stored on an upper shelf, I spied a cracked statuette of some saint in prayer position, and I sighed. "Or, I don't know, maybe the thief is just a sore bingo loser or a clepto who just got a thrill from taking the money but stashed it in the closet later to give it back."

Camille's hands went to her hips and she rolled her eyes.

"Okay, okay," I said. "Forget the Venn diagram thing. Way too complicated." I glanced at the booze bottles. "Why don't we just restock the wine closet and stick a camera in there to see who comes back to play sommelier. If it turns out to be the same person who stole the bingo money and he or she brought it to the church out of guilt, maybe they'll crack and spill their guts as soon as we question them."

"We can't just stick a camera in a closet," Camille said. "Privacy laws, remember?"

Hmm. "Surely the church has a right to its own security. Probably all we need is the priest or someone to okay a monitor of the closet."

Camille looked thoughtful. "*Peut-être.* We can ask, but it could take a while. The priest may not be able to decide a thing like that on his own."

"You mean because it may break some rule like the church as sanctuary or something?"

"That. Plus, red tape. Church bureaucracy can be as bad as the *gouvernement*."

I nodded. She was right. The camera approach could take time and time wasn't on my side if Madame Dumont decided to file a report against me before the long weekend.

I glanced at the booze collection, grabbed a bottle in each hand, and headed into the closet. If Madame Dumont did file a complaint, I didn't want to chance her adding wine theft to my rap sheet.

"Help me get these back, will you?" I asked Camille, explaining about my rap sheet qualms.

She brought over more bottles and set them along the wall just inside the closet door. "*Bonne idée*. But don't bother to hide them again. Let's leave them here. Give the thief something to worry about if he comes back. Let him wonder who moved his stash."

"You know," I said, returning to the hallway. "When the bundle of money fell to the floor, the church ladies saw it happen and turned tail to leave before the bundle was even unwrapped. Don't you think that's odd?"

"All three of them?"

"Yup. And it *is* Madame Dumont who is trying to throw suspicions on me. If Laurent's theory about a magic trick is true, maybe she's the one trying to redirect attention to me and off of her." I paused. "Although I guess that wouldn't explain why all three of the ladies reacted to the bundle find that same way. That doesn't make sense. Unless they're all involved."

Camille stiffened. "*Heille là*, are you including *ma tante* in that all?"

"Of course not," I said.

At least I wasn't including her aloud. Because now that I thought about it, the church was just down the street from the bingo place. It wouldn't take long for someone to pinch the money, stash it in the closet, and be back at bingo without being missed. And Claudette *had* insisted I get the Bunny suit the same night of the bingo. And she *had* shown up at my house at nearly the crack of dawn to see the costume. And she *had* been awfully anxious when she realized I didn't have the feet and insisted we go retrieve them ASAP.

To a budding PI, her behavior could seem a tad suspicious. Maybe even more than a tad. If Claudette wasn't part of the Caron clan, that is. But she was and that gave her automatic immunity, right?

I watched as Camille fastened the padlock on the closet, and I wondered if she'd connected the same dots and dismissed them on the same grounds. And just how much chocolate she'd need to consume before I dared ask her.

OUTSIDE THE CHURCH, I sucked in large cleansing breaths of fresh air as we traipsed across the parking lot to Camille's car.

"Where to next?" Camille said, beeping to unlock her Jetta as we neared its doors.

"I don't know about you," I said. "But I could use a cookie." What I really wanted was a brownie. Or some mint chocolate chip ice cream. But both of those had chocolate and now the mere thought of me consuming anything with chocolate was immediately followed by an image of Claudette waving a no-no finger in my face.

We got in the car and Camille adjusted the sun visor.

"When does this Lent thing end anyway?" I buckled in beside

her and did a mental countdown of days until Easter. "Is it Easter Sunday or Monday?"

"Neither. A lot of places stop on Saturday, but *tante* Claudette's church stops on Thursday evening, the night of the last supper."

I brightened. "Thursday! That's only a day away!"

Camille grinned. "*Mais voyons*, you'd think you were looking forward to its end." She shot me a "mother knows best" style look. "I warned you not to give up chocolate. Lent is not for amateurs."

"Okay, I give. You were right. It *is* hard to go without chocolate. I had no idea it had become such a big part of my life. Next year I'll give up peanut butter like you."

"But you like peanut butter," Camille said on a laugh.

"Not as much as chocolate, apparently. Anyway, we need to stop talking about it. Let's go get something to eat somewhere with no chocolate or peanut butter."

Half a minute passed until we looked at each other, stumped. A place without peanut butter we could probably come up with. A place without chocolate, not so much.

"*Mais alors*," Camille said. "Let's forget about food and get on with finding the money thief so we can prove your innocence. Where was the next place you went after the money was found in the closet?"

"The church kitchen. That's where Laurent took the three Mumketeers for questioning."

"Three Mumketeers?"

"Madame Dumont and Madame Jaffronelli and your aunt," I clarified. "All three of them went mum when Laurent questioned them. At least they did until they starting pointing fingers and one landed on me. Then you came in and know the rest."

"*Okay* then. Maybe it's time we do some snooping on the ladies. Maybe go to the office and do computer checks." Camille's phone trilled in her purse and she got it on the second ring and held it out to me. "*C'est* Adam. For you."

"For me? Why didn't he call me on my mobile?"

"He says he did and you didn't answer."

I rooted in my purse for my phone as I accepted hers. "Hey, Adam. What's up?" My rooting netted me nothing, and I remembered I'd moved my phone to my pocket. I gave the pocket a fast frisking, coming up empty. I extended my search to my seat and its surroundings as I listened to Adam until he abruptly ended our call to get back to Tina.

"*Alors?*" Camille said when I passed back her phone.

"Adam says Tina is still in labor. He said the doctors refused the C-section without medical cause, so Tina's going to deliver instead. He says it could still be hours. Tina's not dilated enough, yet. He'll call when delivery time gets closer."

"*Probablement* Tina is holding the twins in to get her C-section."

I smiled. "I doubt even Tina has the power to pull that off. I'm guessing the babies are scared to come out with all that yelling going on. I could hear Tina screaming in the background demanding her ice chips be made smaller."

Camille went to start the car and her arm bumped mine when I dug my hand into the cup holders between us.

"What are you doing?" Camille said. "You've been fidgeting since Adam called."

"It's my phone. I can't find it."

"Maybe Laurent still has it."

"No. He gave it to me with my purse at the hospital. I put the phone in my pocket and now it's gone." My shoulders slumped as realization hit and I groaned. "It must have fallen out of my pocket when I was searching the closet."

If I'd been on my own, there was a serious possibility that I'd pretend I didn't have the realization and give the phone up for gone. But I wasn't alone, so that wasn't really an option. Plus, Laurent had given me the phone for work, and I doubted he'd buy the gone story. This was the second phone he'd given me, and I was thinking three strikes and I'd be buying the next one on my own dime, and these phones didn't come cheap. There was no way around it. I was going to have to go back to the closet

So I put on my big girl pants and heaved a sigh before getting out of the car and leaning back in when Camille made no move to join me.

"Aren't you coming?" I asked her.

She grabbed for her own phone. *"Mais non. You* have the key and you'll be two minutes. I'll wait here. *D'une façon ou d'une autre,* I have some calls to return."

Translation: Camille was saving her big girl pants for things that didn't include the church closet.

I glanced from her car to the street, rethinking the phone abandonment option. Or better yet, if there was any chance I could skip out altogether and forget about any Lent or Easter Bunny duties I may still have. Or any more dealings with the "Mumketeers" or ferreting out which one of them or their fellow church/bingo ilk may be playing now-you-see-it-now-you-don't magician with the bingo money.

"I wouldn't if I were you," Camille said.

"Wouldn't what?"

She rolled her eyes at me. Best friend or not, sometimes it was eerie the way Camille could read my mind.

I WAS NOSE deep in the church closet when I heard it. My phone ringing. From far in the corner where everything went to die. The ring cutting out before I had a chance to pinpoint it to a precise location.

I backed out and shook my head. Just my luck. I yanked on the light cord and sucked in a big supply of air to ready myself for another plunge into the closet depths for a closer search. This time, my hand grabbing for the padlock before venturing in. Lock me in once, shame on you, lock me in twice, shame on me, and all that. I had no desire to repeat my earlier cloistered closet experience.

The chorus line of wine bottles we'd assembled still sat on the floor and made this shimmy into the corner even tighter than my first. Halfway through, my head tangled in coattails harboring dust mites and tobacco residue. I shuddered and shook the lot off like cobwebs, gingerly sweeping my hand over the floor in search of my phone as I went on. I moved my hand slowly with tiny taps, half afraid something really had died and lurked in the closet depths, even though I'd already searched the place and knew it was free of remains. A gal couldn't be too careful when it came to remains. At least in the PI biz. You never knew when they could turn up.

I had my head turned sideways and an arm thrust behind hanging paraphernalia when I heard my phone ping with text. I veered my hand to the left, tracking the sound before I lost the trail, my fingers finally hitting an edge of smooth, flat, cool glass poking out from broom bristles. I tried to slide the phone to me, but it didn't budge. I sank lower and tried again, this time tugging harder. No go.

I shifted the overhanging garments and reached in again, feeling out the situation, finding broom bristles lodged in the seam along the phone's case cover. The broom handle was tucked behind the clothes rail up top, so I pulled the bottom closer for better inspection and saw the bristle-lock had somehow trapped the phone to a dustpan clamped to the broom's base.

I blew out closet fumes, shielded my nose with an edge of my shirt, and jiggled the broom, prying at the bristles, working fast. A snap sounded, the broom and dustpan separated, neither retaining custody of my phone which skittered to the ground, a white blob plopping onto it.

The shirt end covering my face muffled a tiny squeal when my brain immediately went to church mouse at the sight of the white blob. But the blob didn't move. In fact, it was starting to fill me with a sense of déjà vu. Big time. To just a mere few hours earlier when the bundle of bingo money fell from the Bunny feet. I dropped my face shield, picked up the blob, and loosened a corner of cloth near a blotched seam. A hint of green plastic-like paper came into view and the unmistakable scent of money escaped.

Oh boy. Just what I needed. More money hidden in the closet. Money somehow trapped in the broom, averting my earlier search. Money that would likely have Camille back lobbing nose plugs at me and insisting the closet needed more thorough dredging.

I eyed the new bundle. I had to show it to Camille, right? Because kicking it to the back of the closet and pretending I never saw it would be wrong, right?

I sighed, tucked the bundle in my pocket, reclaimed my phone, and scurried backwards on palms and knees to face the inevitable. I held my breath when I reached the dusty, smoky coattails, and veered to clear the doorway where I slammed into something hard and warm. Something that moved me forward, headfirst, back into the closet. The sound of the door clicking closed reaching my ears just after the light went out.

9

O H NO, THIS could not be happening again. I couldn't be locked in the closet. Not twice in one day. Even *I* couldn't have that kind of bad luck.

No, that was right. This time I couldn't be locked in because this time I had the padlock.

I spat out coattails, clenched the phone in one hand, and snaked my other hand down towards my pocket to be sure the padlock hadn't dropped out. Only my elbow didn't quite bend right to reach the pocket. If it was even possible, my body felt more wedged in than before. Plus, it was hard maneuvering in the dark.

"*Arrête,*" I heard. Deep voice in a near whisper but nearby.

I froze. I wasn't alone.

I opened my mouth to yell and a hand clamped over it. Warm, with enough pressure to seal my lips without causing pain.

"*Calme-toi, mon lapin.*"

At those words, my tension eased as I recognized my closet mate as Laurent, and his hand slipped from my mouth when my body relaxed. I was still on all fours with my head barely clearing

73

the hanging coats, so I resisted the urge to suck in too much air when my mouth was freed. Based on the source of his voice, I was guessing Laurent had to be in a crouch to my side, his knees not far if the hardness poking my thighs was any indication.

"What are you doing in here?" I said. "And why did you push me in?"

"Shush."

Immediately, I tensed again. I hated being shushed. Especially when I didn't know why. And by Laurent who had a habit of shushing me whenever it suited him.

The clippity clop of shoes went by in the hall, and I could have sworn Laurent sucked in a breath. The clippity clop was joined by sharp footsteps, both stopping a bit past the closet, their noise replaced by quiet voices rising and falling. Both French and both female by the sounds of them.

I brought my legs in so I was sitting on my haunches, slowly circled my body to face the closet front, powered on my phone, and tipped it towards Laurent. In the dim light, his scruff darkened his face and accentuated his cheekbones, but it was his eyes I wanted to see, hoping for a clue to explain our impromptu closet coop-up. All I got was a blink when I momentarily lost my balance and accidentally flashed my phone beam in his eyes.

"Oops. Sorry," I mouthed. Then I caught myself. Why was I apologizing? Was it my fault we were sequestered in a closet? Was it my fault the closet was so tiny we were tucked in tighter than beads strung together on a necklace?

Laurent's hand wrapped around my elbow and I steadied, my phone beam floating to the ceiling.

For a minute we stayed like that. Him appearing to listen to the voices in the hall. Me thinking back to the last time I'd been stuck in a closet with a boy. Seventh grade with a guy called Russell, the one and only time I'd played the "seven minutes in heaven" game at a party that turned into several rounds of tic tac toe played on Russell's arm with a pen he carried in his shirt pocket. Which I suspected was how most kids played the closet game but didn't tell anyone.

I eyed Laurent, wondering if he'd ever played the closet game, and if so if tic tac toe had been involved. Then my nose started to crinkle with the stirrings of a sneeze, and Laurent's hand moved from my elbow to lightly pinch my nose, and I decided tic tac toe wasn't Laurent's style. He was far too handy with his body moves. In fact, the closet game may have been when Laurent perfected some of his signature sign language routines. Probably he had a whole storehouse of moves I'd never seen that had little to do with steadying elbows or stifling sneezes.

When Laurent lowered his hand from my nose, I again brought up my shirttail to filter out some of the closet stench beginning to sting the insides of my nostrils from too much exposure. Just when I thought my head might explode from the effort of holding back what would surely have been a humdinger of a sneeze, I started to reach for the doorknob, Laurent clenching my hand mid-reach when more clippity clops came down the hall.

I rolled my eyes and shot Laurent a "this is crazy, I have to get out of here" look. He released my hand, his disappearing in his pocket and resurfacing with one of Camille's chocolates. He held it out to me and I made the sign of the cross with my fingers.

He shook his head at me, peeled off the wrapper, slipped the chocolate in his mouth, and held the empty wrapper up to my nose.

I sucked in a big pull of chocolate fumes before wondering if fumes counted in Lent and deciding they didn't because ingesting was not the same as inhaling, right? And because they did the trick and the burning in my nostrils subsided. So I kept the wrapper in place until finally the clipitty clops in the hall started up again, dimming as they moved away.

Only when it was quiet a full three minutes, did Laurent ease the door open and peek out. He waved the all-clear signal, opened the door wider, and moved into the hall. I scampered out, knees cramping as I forced them back to upright position. I shook my leg to get circulation flowing and the padlock fell out of my pocket and clanked onto the tile floor, followed by the money bundle.

Almost instantly a face poked out of the kitchen doorway. A face framed in a silver updo and sporting a shock of bright red lipstick. Claudette, whose eyes travelled up from the mess on the floor to Laurent and me, then zeroed in on the wrapper in my hand as her reddened mouth pulled into a pinch.

AND WE WERE BACK to the finger wag.

This time, Claudette had Laurent cornered at the end of the hall, leaving me standing near the closet wishing I could read lips. While the church basement acoustics did a swell job of heightening sounds on the tile floor, they did a less swell job with hushed voices. I could make out little of their conversation, and I felt a bit guilty for trying to eavesdrop. But I felt more guilty about Laurent taking the brunt of what I was sure was a finger wag with my name on it since Claudette was hugging the new bingo money find to her chest. And Laurent had nothing to do with the find.

"Sorry to interrupt," I found myself saying, intruding on their *tête-à-tête*. "But Laurent didn't find the bingo money. I did."

Claudette shone her eyes my way, focusing in as though I'd appeared out of thin air. Which I may as well have since I'd been midway down the hall mere seconds ago and felt like my legs must have floated me to the end because I had no memory of directing them to bring me.

A kettle whistled, and Claudette broke her gaze and turned to the kitchen behind her.

I turned, too, noticing only then that we weren't alone. The usual suspects were there. Mesdames Jaffronelli and Dumont. Along with their sentinel, knitting lady, who sat at the head of the long table, knitting needles clicking away. In front of her, a white cloth had money piles set on top spread out like fan blades. The first bingo money find I was guessing if her guarded glare in my direction was any indication.

The kettle whistled again and Madame Jaffronelli got up from her seat at the table and hurried to the stove. Across from her vacated chair, Madame Dumont remained seated. The sooty eyebrows hooding her pinpoint eyes were directed at me, piercing out over glasses, rims as dark as her brows, perfectly perched on the tip of her nose.

A pot of tea appeared on the table courtesy of Madame Jaffronelli, along with dainty porcelain teacups set on dainty porcelain saucers, a mix of floral patterns and colors, faded from decades of repeated washing.

Madame Jaffronelli sat and distributed the hot tea among the cups, tiny wisps of steam rising in front of the seated women and at Claudette's place setting, the room quiet save for a ticking clock on the wall and the occasional click of knitting lady's needles. The stacks of money parked on the white fabric that had swaddled them, more cloth tray now than wrapper, garnered furtive glances from the group but no discussion.

"Come join us," Madame Dumont said in her heavy accent. "We were just about to have tea." Her lips smiled and her teeth nearly gritted as she spoke in a "keep your friends close and your enemies closer" tone. She snapped her fingers towards two free chairs at the table.

I looked at the chairs and felt the sudden urge to flee. I was pretty sure the "enemies" vibe was directed at me. Laurent was likely reading my mind given the slight restraining press of his fingertips on my wrist. He wasn't the sort to run away from a confrontation. I, on the other hand, was ready to don jogging shoes and sprint down the hall for the nearest exit.

"*Oh non, non*. They don't want tea," Claudette said, shuffling the chairs farther down the table side. "They're busy people with busy jobs. They don't have time for tea."

Laurent looked directly at his aunt. "*Oui, ma tante*. We have time for a quick tea. Lora was just saying she could use a break."

I was? Well, a break from the church closet maybe. Or anywhere near the church basement. But I played along. I would have bet four more days of Lent that Laurent had no more of a yearning for tea with the church ladies than I did, so if he was agreeing to it I figured he had his reasons.

"Right," I said, putting on my big girl pants again and directing my feet to stand ground, face my accuser and such. "I wouldn't mind some tea."

Claudette shot her nephew a look that, from the sidelong sparks alone, raised the hairs on the back of my neck.

Laurent ignored the look and sat, sliding the chair beside him over to me using his foot.

A text tone came from my phone as I took my place, and all eyes fell on me.

"Sorry," I said, discreetly checking the message, noting knitting lady had paused her needles and almost hoping she'd treat phone use in the church like she had at the bingo and send me outside to deal with my text. But her needle clicks resumed a second later, and my ping turned out to just be a second notification about the earlier text that had come in while I was in the closet. A note from Camille telling me she was going off to deal with something, but that Laurent was around and would give me a ride home. Which explained why she hadn't come in earlier looking for me, but also meant I was doomed to sit through tea until Laurent was good and ready to leave since I was still on the clock.

I clicked off my phone, set it on vibrate in case anything else came in, and saw that while I'd been occupied reading, Laurent and I had already been given our own teacups and Claudette was seated. With any luck, we'd be done and out of here in no time.

Madame Dumont blew on her tea and took big gulps, ever watchful of me. "*Allez-y*," she said. "*On commence*." She took one last swill of her drink, gyrated the cup, and placed it to sit in front of Claudette.

I sat up straighter in my chair, recognizing the gesture instantly. I'd only been privy to it a few times before, but those times were seared into my memory. Madame Dumont was presenting her tea remnants for a reading.

Beside me, I felt Laurent shift in his chair. Like Camille, Laurent had little belief in tea readings and avoided them when at all possible. About now he was likely regretting prolonging our stay in the church kitchen.

"You didn't tell me this was a reading, *ma tante*," he said. "Maybe Lora and I go and leave you to your friends."

Claudette pivoted her head and fixated on the cupboards over the counters, her nose tipped up just enough to raise her chin and smooth the lines in her neck. Making me think the senior Carons had their own set of sign language cues. This one bordering on "I don't know what you're talking about" territory. When she looked at Laurent again, she moved her hands to her lap and lightened her voice with innocence. "*Mais non*. This is not a tea reading."

"It's true," Madame Jaffronelli piped in from her place down the table, across from me and kitty corner to knitting lady still batting her sticks. "This isn't a tea reading. Well, not a real one. It's only a quick look. Not even a look really. A glance at the leaves, just to, you know, check on things."

Madame Dumont shook her head, tilting the glasses on her nose askew. "Enough talk! We all stay!" She leaned forward and looked at Claudette. "*C'est pas grand chose, Claudette.*" She flicked a crooked finger at the teacup. "*Vas-y.* Just read what it says."

Claudette huffed and leaned in for a look at the leaves in the bottom of Madame Dumont's cup. "*Rien.* It says nothing. *C'est négatif.*"

A smug smile in place, Madame Dumont nodded, crossed her arms over her chest, and sat back.

I had a hard time placing the smug smile. Getting a tea reading of "nothing" didn't sound good to me. It was like hearing you had no future to predict at all.

A knitting needle tapped the table near my cup and I nearly jumped in my seat.

"*Et elle?*" Madame Dumont said.

A flush of heat ran up my spine as memories sparked of the last time Claudette read my leaves and saw danger and talked of soulmates. I didn't need a repeat performance. I had no desire to share my future fortune. I had no desire to hear my future at all! Especially in front of near strangers. Or worse, Laurent. Laurent had a habit of teasing me enough about real events in my life. The last thing I needed was to give him fodder about my supposed future love life.

I put on a smile that could sell teeth whitener. "Oh, please. I'm fine. No need to include me. Someone else can have my turn."

Madame Dumont put on her own toothy smile. Wide and bright, more "big bad wolf" than fresh white gleam. "Nonsense. Everyone must get a turn."

As she spoke, the air in the room seemed to thicken. The other church ladies to still. Like teenagers enduring a Mean Girl stop by at their lunch table in the high school cafeteria. Only these weren't teenagers and this wasn't a cafeteria. These were ladies of the church. Ladies who I was beginning to think may want to oust Madame Dumont from her post for more than just their own chance at movie fame.

I flicked a look at Laurent. Neither one of us the type to cow-tow to power play antics, but both smart enough to know when to play the players. Laurent tipped his head, ever so, briefly, gone as quickly as it came, like a blink. The go-ahead signal letting me know we were on the same page. Unfortunately so, in this case, since that also meant I had to submit to the reading.

I sipped at what was left of my tea and pretend smiled at the faces around the table. All except knitting lady, who had paused her needles during the lull but had since returned her focus to her yarn. With a few bigger gulps, I rendered my tea down to moist leaves and presented them for Claudette's appraisal.

Claudette peered in the cup. For a moment she said nothing, biting into the side of her lip, control at the edges of her eyes.

My heart quickened watching her, praying she wouldn't say anything too embarrassing.

Finally, she shook her head and shoved my teacup aside. "All clear."

There was a collective release of breath from a few of the church ladies. And possibly from me. I didn't understand the read-ing, but at least it was over. No humiliating tidbits of my life revealed for all to hear.

Then it was Laurent's turn. I watched as his saucer was moved to sit in front of Claudette, my pulse quickening again, this time with curiosity.

For Laurent's sake, naturally I hoped nothing embarrassing would come from his reading, either. But a wee part of me was eager for some insider info about the man. After knowing him for a few years and working with him for much of that time, the guy was still a mystery to me. Friendly and joking one minute, quiet and private the next. Hearing his future included winning some game in his hockey league or something didn't so much interest me, but a few insights into the workings of his soul might be nice.

I glanced at Laurent, his face set in that annoying unreadable mode, his hand gripping the teaspoon he'd removed from his cup before passing it to Claudette. He rocked the spoon in his fingers, and I wondered if I was seeing a new entry to his sign language repertoire. Was it possible the big PI boss man was a tad nervous?

I darted a look to Claudette and leaned forward, silently berating myself for my curiosity and near glee at the prospect of learning some deep dark secret about Laurent none of us had any business hearing.

Claudette was biting her lip again, fragments of lipstick coloring her teeth, eventually releasing the bite with another head shake and the return of Laurent's cup.

I slumped in my chair in quasi disappointment as Laurent set his spoon on his saucer, keeping his expression impassive, and Claudette completed reading the rest of the ladies' teacup remnants in turn. Each one resulting in the same head shake.

"*C'est impossible!*" Madame Dumont said, banging an open hand on the table.

Everyone in the group flinched except Laurent, who I was sure had been trained to keep still even if attacked by a swarm of bees or circled by a pack of coyotes.

Claudette regained her composure and heaved a shrug. "*Mais non*. I only see what I see."

Madame Dumont stood and began whisking away the cups, bringing them to the sink. "Then we go again."

"*Non,*" Claudette said.

"*Oui!*" Madame Dumont said.

I looked at Laurent in confusion. This wasn't like Claudette's other tea readings. No big pronouncements about anyone's future. No cliffhanger implications about anyone's fate. No warnings. Nothing. And now this argument. I didn't get it.

Madame Dumont came to sweep more cups from the table and stopped near Claudette.

"*Tu n'as pas lu les tiennes,*" Madame Dumont said.

I checked Laurent for a clue, not understanding the words and even more confused, but Laurent's focus was on the action.

Claudette stood, snatching her own cup from its saucer. "I can't read my own tea." She tutted at Madame Dumont in what came off as church lady "duh," and she moved to the sink.

Judging by the scowl Madame Dumont took on, Claudette's response didn't quite cut it for her, but it cleared up their exchange for me. Seemed Claudette hadn't been included in the "*everyone gets a tea reading*" turn thing and Madame Dumont was miffed about it.

The two women batted more words back and forth in French, falling silent when two men walked into the room. One man had a rake in hand, the other a broom. Both were seniors I recognized from bingo night. Rakeman the guy with the dancing eyebrows. Broomman the wiry guy who gave Rakeman the wad of tickets when I was outside on my phone call with Adam.

Broomman walked over to Madame Jaffronelli and pecked a kiss on her cheek.

Rakeman directed his attention to Madame Dumont. "*De café?*"

She barked out some French words, and Rakeman plopped himself in the seat beside mine. He smelled of grass and sweat and church closet, and his bones creaked when they hit the chair.

Madame Dumont set a fresh teapot in front of him along with a cup then added leftover pastries from bingo night and some tiny plates to the table and resettled herself, shifting to make room for Broomman to sit between her and Madame Jaffronelli.

Broomman surveyed the pastries, rubbing at some grime on his hands with a handkerchief, then started filling his plate.

Rakeman wasted no time grabbing a few choice pastries for himself and leaning into me. "I hear you are our new Easter Bunny," he said, touching his elbow to mine, enunciating each word slowly, his French accent as thick as Madame Dumont's. Not a surprise since I was guessing she was his wife and likely his informant about both my Easter Bunny stint and my English status.

I nodded and held in a sigh as the carpet Bunny flashed in my mind. Despite Madame Dumont's misgivings about me, she hadn't relieved me of my Bunny duties, yet. A fact that both surprised and disappointed me, since not wearing the costume would be the one perk of this whole mess.

The new arrivals grinned at each other a beat and each took a swig of their tea then started in on the pastries, and chatter broke out around the table. Among everyone except Laurent and me. And knitting lady who had yet to say a word as her needles clacked away at what was slowly taking shape as a bulky sweater woven with multicolored yarn, one completed sleeve resting on the table in front of her.

The table I now noticed was minus the stacks of money there just moments ago. Disappeared from sight so quickly, I wondered if knitting lady's needles doubled as magic wands. And if maybe *she* could be our magician.

10

"*D*ID YOU SEE that?" I asked Laurent when we'd settled into the privacy of his car. "The money disappeared just like that." I snapped my fingers. "And I bet I know where it went. Straight into the sentinel's knitting bag."

Laurent's eyebrow arched at me.

"The sentinel," I said again. "You know, the lady who's always knitting?"

"Giselle Montagne?"

"Is that her name? Well, yeah, her. She was in charge of the money at the bingo, too."

Laurent eased the car out of the church lot. "Giselle is treasurer for the group."

Ah, the treasurer. That explained her ties to the money. But she had a heck of a management style. Fanning the money out like a display. Not to mention her frequent knitting needle tapping. "She doesn't say much."

"I wouldn't know. I try to keep clear of *ma tante's* group."

Hmm. "Is that what you were doing in the closet? Keeping clear?"

Laurent adjusted his mirror and made a lane change before answering. "That was more to keep *you* clear."

"Me? You mean because Madame Dumont thinks I'm a thief?"

"Something like that."

I watched a line of bicyclists go by along the bike lane beside me, wondering again how I'd managed to get myself into this bingo money mess and just what it would take to clear my name. The circumstances were so ridiculous I knew it would all blow over eventually, but eventually couldn't come soon enough for me.

"If you wanted to keep me clear, why did you agree to stay for tea?" I asked Laurent.

"You'd just found more money. Better you stay and face your accuser than run and look guilty."

I hadn't thought of that angle, but it kinda made sense.

"If I'd known it was a tea reading, I would have gladly run and looked guilty," I said. "What was up with that? All that 'nothing"'and 'all clear' business. That's not what my other tea readings with Claudette were like."

"*Non?* What happened at those?"

I fiddled with my seat belt. "Nothing. Well, I mean not nothing like today's nothing. Just nothing important. Just crazy predictions." A few of which may have come true, but telling Laurent about those would mean giving more details, and I wasn't about to tell him Claudette had also predicted me meeting my soulmate and implied said soulmate was not Adam. Especially when Laurent's tea reading hadn't included any personal tidbits at all. I certainly wasn't going to be the only one sharing fortune telling prophesies, true or not.

"Anyway," I continued, "this reading today was very different.

We're lucky those guys came in when they did or I'm guessing we'd have had to sit through a repeat round."

Laurent slid a look my way. "*Oui. Puis* you made a new friend. You and Monsieur Dumont are rubbing elbows already."

I grimaced at the memory. "He was very friendly, wasn't he? But I doubt his wife was happy about him chatting up her suspect. Plus, I hate to say it, but he smelled like that stinky closet."

"*Ben*, that's because he's the custodian for the church. His buddy, Monsieur Jaffronelli also helps, but Monsieur Dumont has worked there so long I don't remember him not being there. I think *ma tante* said once that's how the Dumonts met."

My phone rang with a call from Adam as I was about to respond, and I hit the pause button on my thought while I picked up.

"Tina had the babies!" Adam shouted at me over infant cries as we connected. "Two perfect boys. Five pounds two ounces, five pounds three ounces. Both over nineteen inches long. Which I know sounds small, but trust me it's good for twins."

Laurent flashed me a thumbs up from the steering wheel. He'd heard everything, of course, given the shouting.

"That's great," I told Adam. "How's Tina?"

"Amazing. Tired but amazing. She let me stay in the delivery room with her and Jeffrey. I saw everything. It was intense."

"I bet."

"Can you swing by the house on your way over?" he asked. "In all the rush this morning I didn't bring my gifts for the twins. They're in my office by the sofa-bed."

"Sure. No problem. I'm headed home now to put Pong out."

Laurent met my eyes on that. We hadn't really discussed a destination when we'd left the church. Both of us more focused on the "leaving" than the "going to" of our escape.

"I'll be at the hospital as soon as I can," I added to Adam, hoping he heard me over the intensifying cries on his end.

"*My* gifts?" Laurent said when I ended the call. "You and Adam got separate gifts for the babies?"

Hmm. Adam had said that, hadn't he? Leave it to a PI to pick up on that bit. "I'm sure it was just a slip of the tongue in all the excitement."

Then remembering Camille had bought something from the gift shop for me to give as well, I dialed her and made a mental note to add Adam's name to that card to avoid any other confusion.

"*Un instant,*" Camille's voice came to me over the phone then went mute before coming back.

"Where are you?" I said after telling her about the babies coming.

Her answer came fast but was broken up. I couldn't make it all out, so I explained about the gift and asked if she could swing by and meet me in maternity.

A slight pause came before she agreed. Then I told her about the new money find in the closet "ATM" and she went quiet a beat again. But this time I heard a faint tapping sound in the background, and she sounded distracted as she came back on the line. "Be there in an hour," she assured me. "Bring the Bunny suit." And she clicked off.

COULD THIS DAY get any weirder? Not even in a crazy dream could I imagine myself trudging through a hospital corridor carrying twin gift bags tied with helium "It's a boy!" balloons in one arm and a scruffy Bunny suit in the other.

Laurent had insisted he drive me over so I could avoid parking hassles, and we'd parted at the side door where he'd dropped me off. I had barely five minutes to get to the gift shop where Camille and I had agreed to meet downstairs and go up together. Finding my way through the maze of hallways with only French signage for direction and weighed down by my various accoutrements had me thinking I'd be late.

"*Heille! Finalement!*" Camille called, hurrying towards me as I rounded a bend.

I glanced at the wall clock nearby. "I'm only five minutes late. You can't have been waiting that long."

She slid the gift bag handles off my arm and slipped them onto her own, stringing them with the bags she'd brought, and she passed me a takeout coffee and looped her free arm through mine. "Five minutes, *c'est une éternité à l'hôpital!*"

I guess for someone who hated hospitals as much as Camille that was true.

She steered us over to a metal bench tucked along a wall tiled in tiny blue squares. A teenage boy sat to one side of the bench, man spread style, a look of pure boredom on this face. Camille shot him a look. He got up and wandered away, and Camille parked our bags in his place.

She sank down to sit beside the bags. "Come sit. I need a minute before we go up."

I joined her and tilted my body slightly, as she had, so we were partially facing each other. I watched her take a big drag on her own takeout coffee and use her hand to fan small pink spots creeping onto her cheeks.

I took a sip of my coffee. Tepid. Likely the same as hers and likely not the cause of her pink cheeks. The pink, I was guessing, was hospital anxiety setting in. Or Tina anxiety. I could go either way on that.

"Thanks for bringing the gift," I told her. "But you don't have to come up. I can visit Tina and the babies on my own and go home with Adam."

The pink lessened a notch and Camille paused her coffee gulps to pull out a lipstick and compact from her purse and touch up her lips. "Don't be ridiculous. *Naturellement* I'm going up with you." She stowed the makeup away, extracted a comb, and smoothed her hair.

With her bag open, I noticed a white bundle jutting out. A bundle that looked suspiciously familiar.

"Is that what I think it is?" I asked, pointing to the bundle.

Camille smiled. "It is if you think it's the second wad of money from the closet."

"How did you get it?"

"*Tante* Claudette."

"I'm confused. Didn't she give it to the sentinel knitting lady, er, the treasurer, Giselle?

Camille cocked her head at me, and I explained Laurent had filled me in about Giselle. Also, I told her about my suspicions that knitting lady could be our magician.

"*C'est possible. En tout cas*, Claudette never showed this money to the group."

"How come?"

Camille rolled her eyes at me. "*Mais voyons*, she's not going to let Madame Dumont see it and tell her you found it. It would make you look bad. *Ma tante* would never do that to you."

I felt a warm bubble tingle in my chest. Was it possible I'd been wrong and Claudette didn't doubt me? Her gesture touched and heartened me. Only I didn't want it to get her into trouble. "But what about her group? She has to tell them. She can't hold back something like that. It could hurt her standing or her run for group head."

Camille shook her head at me. Like I was a bit slow on the

uptake. Or worse, insulting her aunt's judgment. Then she checked the time on her phone, clicked her purse closed, and stood. "Oh, it's late. We have ten minutes to visit the new family and then we go." She took a few steps and turned back to me, gesturing at the flattened furry carpet mess sheathed in plastic folded on my lap. "You brought the Bunny suit?"

"Yup." I felt my shoulders droop at the costume reference. The mere thought of it bringing on an Easter funk. "Please tell me you're taking it back."

"*Non, non*. You need it for the dress rehearsal." Her eyes grew bigger and she waved an arm at me like I wasn't getting up fast enough. "Come on already. I'm good now. We have to go."

I leaned into the bench and crossed my arms. "Oh no you don't. You can't just drop the words 'dress rehearsal' and take off. Exactly where do we have to go?"

"*Mais voyons*. I just told you. The dress rehearsal for the Easter play."

I stared at her, waiting for more.

Camille gave an exaggerated sigh and resumed her seat. "Isn't Adam waiting for you upstairs?"

I nodded. Since she already knew the answer to her query, it was less a question and more a stall tactic. Camille wasn't fooling me. She hadn't just come to the hospital to meet me with the baby gift. She had something else in mind. Something she didn't want to tell me just yet. Maybe something she thought I wouldn't want to hear. And if that something had to do with me and the Bunny suit she was right. But I was sensing that not knowing was not going to save me from whatever scheme Camille had in mind, so probably I should get the knowing over with already. Fast. Like ripping off a band-aid.

I hesitated. Who was I kidding? That was a bad example. I *never* ripped off a band-aid. I dampened it with warm water to dissolve the glue holding the bandage then I eased it off. Slow and steady and relatively pain-free.

Which is exactly what I needed to do now with whatever this business was, ease into it, one fragment at a time.

"Okay," I said. "Tell me about this rehearsal."

"Tonight is the full dress rehearsal for the kids' play. And *Les Femmes de l'Église* women will all be there. Also their cronies. Which is pretty much the same crowd as for the bingo. They're all playing audience so the kids get the full feel of the run-through."

"Okay," I said, unclear where she was going.

"For you, too, it's a rehearsal," Camille said. "Julie wants you there also."

"Julie?"

"The head Sunday school teacher. She was there with the kids for the practice this morning. You saw her. The woman in the jogging suit."

Right. The woman trying to corral the kids onstage.

"What does she want me there for?"

"So you'll know what to do tomorrow at show time. She wants to talk to you about what you'll need to do and introduce you to the kids."

"I don't get it. If I'm suspect numero uno in their bingo woes, why do the church ladies even still want me involved?"

"The church ladies have nothing to do with it. It's Julie who wants you there."

"Why?" I said. "Julie doesn't even know me."

"*Mais non.* But she knows you fit the Easter Bunny costume and the Easter Bunny is part of the play."

I blinked. "What do you mean part of the play? I thought I was just helping with the kids offstage and playing Bunny on Sunday to give out chocolate eggs."

"*Oui, oui,* you are. But you're also in the play tomorrow."

My heart skipped a beat. This was getting worse and worse. Now I wasn't just helping with the play. I had to be in it!

"Nobody told me I was *in* the play." I stopped talking, frozen to the bench as memories of my awful drama class days from high school came back to me. "How many lines do I have? I don't have time to learn lines!"

"*T'inquiète pas.* You only have two lines."

My pulse started drumming in my ears. "Two! That means I have to learn cues, too. I'm terrible at cues!"

Camille tapped her foot on the floor. "*Voyons*, it's just a kids' play, Lora. You only speak at the end. Two easy lines. That's it. No big cues to learn. Just one. You just enter in the final scene and greet the kids."

The rush of blood to my ears slowed. "Oh. You mean like Santa arriving on his sleigh at the end of a Christmas parade and waving to the kids. I can do that."

"*C'est certain* you can do that." Camille took my elbow and tried to ease me off the bench. "But we have to hurry or we'll be late. Laurent will be waiting."

I started to get up and gather my stuff. "Laurent? What's he got to do with it?"

Camille tossed her empty coffee cup in a nearby garbage, and we headed for the elevators.

"Julie wants to tape the rehearsal to show the kids so they can see how it looks and fix any mistakes before the real performance. Laurent volunteered to take the video."

Hmm. There had to be more to it than that. Camille wouldn't care about being late for some rehearsal. And Laurent's strategy to steer clear of his aunt's group would not include taking videos of their play. There was something Camille still wasn't telling me In my mind's eye, I pictured my band-aid only halfway off, still clinging to my skin, stuck solid like it had been applied with some kind of superglue on one side.

The elevator came and Camille and I were moved in, swept along by the waiting crowd, separated as we got on among the passengers. Winding our way back together when we exited on the maternity floor.

I pulled her aside before we headed to Tina's room and continued our conversation as though it had been on a temporary pause just waiting for the "play" button to start again.

"Why is Laurent taping the rehearsal? What aren't you telling me?"

She sighed and moved us to the same chair area down the hall from Tina's room where we'd been holed up earlier in the day.

She tapped her purse. "It's simple. After you say your lines and start to do your dance, you'll drop this money bundle out of your Bunny suit. And Laurent will be there to record the crowd for reaction."

The drum beat returned to my ears. There was so much to unpack in those two sentences I almost didn't know where to start. "Excuse me? What dance?"

Camille heaved a sigh. "*Voyons*, Lora. The Easter Bunny *always* does a dance in the play," she said like this was common knowledge. "It's nothing. The important part is you dropping the money. Since most of the bingo crowd will be there, probably the thief will be there, too. And he may not even know the money is missing yet. If he sees it with you he will be very surprised."

"So this is some kind of plan? I'm supposed to annoy the thief into confessing? I don't think that will work. Who came up with this lame plan, anyway?"

She narrowed her eyes at me. "*Heille là*, it's not me who decided to play Easter Bunny. We wouldn't have been anywhere near the bingo if we didn't have to pick up your costume and all this wouldn't be our problem and we wouldn't need a plan to fix it."

Okay then. So it was Camille's plan. Plus, she had a fair point. I still didn't think this idea would get us anywhere, but I was in no position to complain. As she so eloquently pointed out, I was at the center of the mess.

"All right," I said. "Where will you be during all this?"

"Me, I'll be waiting at the church to see if anyone goes to the closet to check on the bingo loot. If we get lucky, when the thief sees your bundle, he'll get worried enough to double check his stash, hoping yours just coincidentally looks like his. Then I'll know who it is."

Hmm. "What if the thief is the same person who locked me in the closet? The thief could have anger management issues. What if he or she spots the bundle and doesn't bother with the worry stage and goes straight to anger. I don't want to be the focus of that anger. I'll give you that we need to do something, but I'm not sure I'm liking this plan."

"We only have a day to solve the case before Madame Dumont reports you for the theft. We don't even have a real list of suspects. Or time to investigate them properly if we did." Camille shrugged. "We have to do something to flush out the real thief. You got any better ideas?"

"Sure. *You* parade around the rehearsal with the bundle, and *I'll* wait at the closet to see if anyone shows up."

"*Vraiment*, Lora? You want to wait at the closet by yourself? You hate the closet."

This was true. But the idea of dancing around in the carpet Bunny costume ran a close second in that department. Okay maybe hate was a bit much. The Bunny suit was more cringe-worthy than hate-worthy.

"This whole thing is becoming ludicrous," I said. "And I still don't get why the church ladies don't just replace me if they think I'm some kind of thief."

Camille started to give me the same answer as always, and I held up a hand. "I know, I know. You told me already. Because I fit the costume. But there have to be lots of parishioners who would fit the Bunny suit. Why don't they just ask one of them?"

Camille let out a laugh and rolled her eyes. "None of them would do it. They all saw what the kids did to last year's Bunny. They aren't going to volunteer for that!"

"*Excuse me?* What happened to last year's Bunny?"

Camille grabbed our gift bags and headed off for Tina's room, calling over her shoulder, "You don't want to know."

11

*T*INA'S TWINS WERE beautiful. If it's okay to call boy babies beautiful. Which in this case it had to be because these boys seemed to bypass the cute newborn stage and go directly to the sculpted cheek bones and jaw lines stage. Each with big eyes and lots of eyebrow and dark hair that already seemed coiffed to tuck behind their ears with just one roaming lock sitting on each forehead.

"Lora!" Tina trilled when she saw me. "Come see my wonderful boys!"

With Adam and Jeffrey flanking Tina, partially raised in her bed, each infant nestled on a pillow tucked in on either side of her ribcage, her arms outstretched to encircle both babies, she was indeed surrounded by several boys, and could have been referring to any of them.

"Wait!" she ordered as Camille and I began crossing the room and stopped in our tracks.

Tina gave a big smile and the room filled with a series of clicks. I shifted my attention from the babies to notice large, white umbrella-like stands at the foot of Tina's bed and a man, one knee slightly bent forward, snapping pictures of the new family.

As the man stopped clicking, straightened, and reached to close one of the umbrellas, I tentatively moved closer to the bed.

"Are you sure you got enough?" Tina said, fixing the man with a doubtful gaze. "Maybe we should take a few more in the cradle position?"

The man shook his head and assured her they had taken more than enough. By his frantic collection of his things, I was guessing "more than enough" probably meant he could fill a coffee-table book with the number of pictures he'd taken and was hurrying to escape before the book got turned into a series.

"Look what I got!" Tina said when he left. She jiggled the pillows propping up the babies. The baby on her left grimaced and the baby on her right fluttered his lashes. Easy to see which boy would take after Tina.

I went to Adam's side, Camille hovering behind me.

"They're beautiful," I said, glancing from the babies to Tina and Jeffrey, each parent beaming.

Adam dropped a kiss on the top of my head. "They are, aren't they?"

"Almost makes you want one," Camille said.

I slid her a look.

She met my eyes and her brows furrowed. "*Pas moi mais* just some 'you' somewhere."

I smiled. Camille had been seeing the same man for several months, a guy she met on a case, and they'd been "unofficially" living together for a while. The guy was more than happy to make it official, Camille less so. Camille was beginning to accept the concept of a "relationship" in her life so long as there were no external signals the world may mistake for long-term commitment. A baby screamed long-term commitment—to the child and to the baby-daddy for all to see. Camille admitting she may want a baby was like admitting she actually liked chain store shopping. Not going to happen any time soon.

"Did you name the babies, yet?" I asked.

Jeffrey nodded. "We've narrowed it down to Dylan and Thomas or Huck and Finn. After either Tina's favorite poet or literary character."

Camille glanced at me, likely as surprised as I was to hear Tina knew much about literature, let alone had favorite literary-inspired names. It was rare to even see her with a book.

"What do you think, hon?" Adam said. "I'm voting for Huck and Finn. That little fella there looks like a Finn, don't ya think?"

"I guess," I said, looking at the fella in question, the baby with the fluttery eyelashes.

"I don't know," Tina said, letting her head lull on a pillow wadded at her neck and twisting her lips to the side, flattening the opposite cheek. She tapped the baby on the left with her fingers. "I think this little guy looks more like a Dylan."

"Isn't Dylan a girl's name?" Camille said.

I jabbed her in the ribs, wishing for that "rewind and edit" function on her mouth I thought would be handy to have now and then.

Tina's eyes flared and mine pinched closed in a long blink, opening to catch Tina and Jeffrey sharing a long look.

"Dylan is unisex," I told Camille. Then hoping to bring focus back to the new parents, I turned to them. "I think both sets of names are great. Very clever. And a fun idea to go with pairs." I laughed. "Probably if I was trying to come up with a name that would work like that I'd think Anderson Cooper."

Jeffrey and Tina exchanged another look, Tina gnawing at her lower lip as her eyes flitted from one baby to the other, and circled back to Jeffrey, her lips morphing into a pout.

Jeffrey turned to me. "Would you mind, Lora?"

"Excuse me?"

"Anderson and Cooper are perfect names. Would you mind if we used them?"

"Seriously?" I asked, surprised Tina would want any name suggestions from me, intentional or otherwise. Especially when she already had her own names narrowed down.

Jeffrey nodded and I followed suit.

"Absolutely," I said. "I mean, go ahead. The names are all yours." Well, technically they belonged to the actual Anderson Cooper. At least they did when they were put together. Separately I guess they were just ordinary names free for the taking. I suspected Tina may not even know the person they did belong to. Probably she just liked the sound of them.

A tear rolled down Tina's cheek and she shifted one hand to reach for mine and give it a squeeze, her lower lip trembling now.

I smiled at her, sure I was witnessing another bout of pregnancy hormones. They'd overtaken Tina at times over the last few months, allowing her uncharacteristic moments of true vulnerability, and dare I say, maybe glimpses at her sweet side.

"Excellent!" Jeffrey announced as we all cooed over the babies some more, marveling at their little hands and sweet smell and gobs of hair. Then Camille elbowed *me* in the ribs, her eyes travelled over to the wall clock, and she began inching for the door.

I shot her a side-eye. I hadn't even had a chance to hold either of the babies yet. Surely it couldn't already be time to go.

"Is that for the boys?" Tina asked, finally managing to find her voice again and coyly pointing to the furry mass draped over my arm.

I nearly jumped at the sight of it, forgetting I was still holding the rabbit suit, which under the glare of hospital lights could pass for a stuffed toy. Or a puppet maybe.

Camille slowed her beeline for the exit, and I considered the merits of taking advantage of the occasion to tell Tina that yes, in fact, the costume was a gift for the babies and ditch the suit here and now. Without the suit, I wouldn't have to do the Easter Bunny dance at the rehearsal, right?

I stifled a sigh, knowing I'd never get away with leaving the costume behind even if I did muster up the courage to go through with it. "Uh, no. But these are!" I added a flourish and gestured at the gift bags and balloons we *had* brought for the babies.

Adam claimed the smaller bags featuring a cow and moon scene and he presented them for opening.

"Oh, Adam," Tina giggled. "More presents? First the twin stroller and now these? You're spoiling me."

Ah, the twin stroller. Adam had been debating between that and expanding cribs for some time. He'd finally gone with the stroller as a way to get something both babies could share. Some high-end designer pram big with celebrity mommies. I'd chipped into that and thrown Tina's baby shower, which had me thinking we were good on the big gift giving, so I was surprised when Tina pulled a sterling silver brush and comb set from a bag. Followed by a second matching set from the other bag.

Tina squealed and the babies fussed briefly. "Omigod. These are beautiful."

Adam leaned in and pointed to the brush handle on the closest set. "And see this spot here? That's where I'm having their names engraved. That way you won't mix up whose is whose."

Camille had ventured to my side for a peek and she rolled her eyes at me. Probably thinking the same as I was. That probably the siblings didn't need two sets. Probably the boys could take turns having their locks combed.

Tina went on to open the rest of our gifts. The haul Camille had pulled together from the gift shop. Lots of blue clothes and bibs and two very cute Winnie the Pooh bowl sets. But nothing in sterling silver.

As Tina fell quiet and her eyes began to close, Jeffrey thanked everyone for the lot and moved the coiffing tools from Tina's chest, where she'd set them while she went through the other gifts. When her breathing slowed, Jeffrey and Adam each lifted a sleeping baby from the bed and set them in their little hospital bassinettes. Leaving them looking even more adorable and me with no excuses left to prolong our visit.

I said my goodbyes to Jeffrey and signaled Adam to meet me in the hall where I told him about the play rehearsal. For a moment, I debated filling him in on Camille's scheme, but that would mean also telling him the rest of the events surrounding the bingo money theft, and I didn't have the heart to darken Adam's day of becoming a godfather with the craziness of my day.

"Give me a minute and I'll go with you," Adam surprised me by saying.

I skimmed my eyes to Camille standing by the elevators, flicking her gaze between the doors and her phone screen. Probably she wouldn't mind if Adam tagged along to the rehearsal. I, on the other hand, wasn't so sure. Then he'd see me in the carpet Bunny suit doing whatever silly dance I was supposed to do. And accidentally on purpose dropping the bingo bundle. That could make it hard to avoid telling him about all the bingo craziness and my current status with Madame Dumont as suspect number one in the money theft.

Before I had a chance to answer, Adam dipped into Tina's room and was back wearing his jacket and carrying a charger in his hand.

The elevator doors opened and we all got in, Adam noticing me noticing his charger.

"It's for my phone. It's worn down from covering the twins'

birth. I'm gonna need to charge it in the car on the way to the rehearsal. It's not everyday my girlfriend helps with an Easter play." He smiled at me. "I may want to take a few pictures or even some video."

I cringed. Just what I needed. To spend my evening with not just one man in my life taking video of me dancing in the wretched costume, but two.

12

*S*ERIOUSLY, WAS CHOCOLATE the only prop in this play? Everywhere I looked onstage, baskets were filled with chocolate eggs, miniature chocolate bunnies were set on tables, little chocolate chicks were displayed atop shredded paper hay. I get it, chocolate and Easter are fast friends. But there are other Easter symbols. Like bonnets or dyed eggs. Where were the bonnets and colored eggs?

I cinched the slit closed on the backstage curtain shielding me, and I shook my head at Camille in no uncertain terms. "Nuh uh. I am not going out there looking like this. There are at least sixty people out there." Not to mention the chocolate. I had immense doubts about my Lent discipline amidst all that chocolate if I had to parade around in the Bunny suit, too. A gal can only make so many sacrifices at a time, and wearing the suit in front of a roomful of people definitely involved sacrificing my dignity.

Camille forced a smile at a father passing by towing his kid by the hand. One of the girls in tutus who looked about as keen as I did about going onstage.

"*Voyons*, Lora," Camille whispered to me, dropping the smile. "You're supposed to be helping with the kids. Not acting like one. Get a hold of yourself. You're the grownup here, remember?"

I huffed at her. "I thought when I'd be helping, I'd *look* like a grownup. Not some Bunny in need of a pedicure, a shower, and a serious hair conditioning treatment." I scratched at the side of the Bunny head. "And this head is hot. It's like a hundred and fifty degrees in here."

"*Mais là*, that's not the head. It's the heat. It's cranked up again."

"Mademoiselle Weaver?" someone called.

I swiveled my head in the direction of the voice, losing my narrow view out the tiny eye holes in the Bunny face when it didn't move with me.

I felt a hand gently pump my paw in a handshake and heard a faint rustling of paper. "I'm Julie. The Sunday school teacher. I can't thank you enough for filling in as our Bunny. A new parishioner was all set to do it and then suddenly decided to take her spring vacation over Easter. We were really scrambling to find a last minute replacement when Claudette recommended you. I'm so glad you could make time for us. What a stroke of luck she knew a social worker already vetted to work with kids. We really didn't have time to run anyone new through the system for approval."

Julie dropped my paw, and I discreetly brought it upwards to realign the Bunny head with my face. Julie was tall and sturdy as a farmhand with a pleasant roundness around her middle. She had no discernible accent when she spoke and addressed me in English, giving me the sense she was fully bilingual, making at least part of my Bunny duties easier. And since clearly Claudette had used my previous career credentials to vouch for me, Julie seemed keen to have me on board.

"No problem," I said. "Glad to help." I would have preferred that help be sans Bunny suit, but the basic sentiment was true. I *was* glad to help, and Camille was right. I had to get over myself and woman up. I may not have volunteered for all the associated mess with the missing bingo money, but the play wasn't about that. The play was for the kids. Plus, if Camille's quirky plan worked, I'd be off the hook with Madame Dumont soon. Anything I had to do to make that happen was worth a little time in the suit.

Julie toyed with a dog-eared booklet on a clipboard and formed a shy smile. "I understand it may be hard for you to prompt the kids with their lines, so for tonight if you could just watch until it's time for your entrance." She flipped the booklet open to a page marked with a yellow stickie and pushed the booklet into my paw. "It's here, right after the dinner scene."

I clenched the booklet tight to keep it from slipping from the carpet fur.

She added a sheet of paper and tapped it in the center. "And these are the words for your song." Julie glanced at Camille. "If you go over them together beforehand the pronunciations should be easy."

"Song?" I said, the Bunny head deepening the word in my ears.

"Right. You sing it while you do the dance. The kids love it."

One of said kids tugged at the hem of Julie's smock, and Julie excused herself to address whatever crisis the kid whispered at her.

I pulled Camille close to me. "Song! Song!" I said. "You didn't tell me I'd have to sing a song. In French no less!"

Camille shrugged. "I didn't remember the song." She snatched the paper from my paw and gave the lyrics a once-over. "*Ah oui.* I remember now. It's not a real song. It's just the Frère Jacques song with some different words for *Pâques*." She sang a bit for me. "See, it's easy. I'll teach it to you for tomorrow. Today you can just hum. The kids will be humming the music and they hum loud, so you'll blend in. No one will notice you're not singing. And the dance you can just make up to go with the music." She shoved the paper back with the play booklet. "Just make sure you cover the whole stage as you dance. Let the bundle drop near the end of the song and keep moving."

I looked at the giant Bunny feet and their protruding stick toes. "I don't know if I can dance in this thing. I may have to stop moving and just sway or something."

"*Non, non.* Never stop moving."

I fixed her with a dubious glare, a move wasted on Camille since my eyes were barely visible through my peepholes. "Why?"

"Just don't."

I felt a hand on my shoulder. "*Ben*, don't what? Don't tell me our little *lapin* has hopped into more trouble already."

"Good, you're here." I said, swiveling towards Laurent's voice, trying to guide the Bunny head along with mine and failing. Shifting a giant Bunny head with papers clutched in my paw evidently didn't go smoothly.

Through the one working eye opening, Laurent's arms came into view. I felt fabric rustle my scalp, the Bunny eye holes aligned closer to my peepers, and all of Laurent became visible.

"Maybe you can tell me why I'm supposed to stay in motion onstage," I said to him. "Your sister here insists I do, but she's more vague on why."

Laurent's gaze moved to his sister. "You didn't tell her?"

"There's nothing to tell, big brother," Camille said.

I couldn't turn fast enough to see it, but I could tell by her tone she'd added a squint to her reply. A squint was not good.

I tucked the booklet under an arm and planted a hand atop the Bunny head, holding it in place, eyeholes aligned, so I could pivot for a look at Camille to confirm the squint.

"Look," I said, moving closer when a trio of woodsmen boys

ran by us towards the stage. "One of you had better tell me or I'm *not* going out there."

"It only matters tomorrow," Camille said. "Today is just rehearsal. We'll go over it when you learn the song."

I shook my head and felt a Bunny ear droop. "Nuh, uh. I want to know now."

Laurent's hands came to my shoulder and he guided me to the curtain slit to the stage. "See that dark spot on the floor?" he asked me.

I panned the stage, barely seeing floor at all, most of it blocked by the table and tree props and kids.

Laurent crouched to my height, straightened, and pulled a kid-sized chair in from the wings. He gestured at the chair. "Try now."

I stepped up and with the added height, I spotted a black area on the ground maybe the size of a jumbo pizza. "I see a black circle if that's what you mean."

He helped my giant Bunny feet descend the chair. "*Ben* that's it. That's your burrow. At the end of the play, the kids chase you for the eggs and try to keep you from reaching your burrow and disappearing into the hole."

I blinked at him. "There's a hole on the stage?" I scratched at the Bunny head, growing even warmer. Now I had to dance around a stage in clumsy, giant Bunny feet *and* casually drop the money bundle *and* avoid accidentally falling in a hole? All while a pack of kids chased me?

"I can see why you didn't want to tell me," I said to Camille. "This is getting worse by the minute." I felt more heat prickle up my spine. "Oh no. Is that why no one else wants to play Easter Bunny? Did last year's Bunny fall in the hole and break all his bones or something?"

Camille waved her hand at me like I was being ridiculous. "*Non, non*. It's not a real hole, Lora. Just paint to look like a hole. When the Easter Bunny reaches the paint circle and balls up small on the floor, it looks to the audience like the Bunny is gone. Only the kids see the spot well. The hole is not the problem. It's the chasing that did in last year's Bunny. Some of the kids chase, and some of them block the Bunny from the burrow because once the Bunny reaches the burrow, the chase is over and the Bunny is safely home and the kids get no more *chocolat*. Last year's Bunny was too slow and by the time she got to the hole, the kids had pulled off the costume in the chase and the Bunny was left wearing nothing but underwear and bruises and rabbit ears in front of the priest and the whole congregation." Camille paused for a breath. "But you don't have to worry about any of that today because today you have no *chocolat*. Today is just a rehearsal chase for the kids to run around and *pretend* to block you."

"What about tomorrow at the performance?"

"Then you have the *chocolat*. But not to worry, I have a plan for tomorrow."

"I see Adam has come to see the show," Laurent interjected. He was at the curtain slit again, peering out. "It looks like he's taking pictures with his phone."

I moved in beside Laurent, stepped back up on the kiddie chair, and scanned the audience for Adam. "Which reminds me," I said. "Aren't you supposed to be taping the rehearsal?"

"*Oui*. I'm taping now." Laurent pointed in the vicinity of the table where knitting lady sat by her cash box. To her left, was a tripod holding a camera.

"Isn't that cheating?" I said.

Laurent smiled. "That's second crew." He tapped the rear pocket in his jeans that held his phone. "When you go out, it's first crew that will film."

I located Adam sitting on the aisle, three rows behind Mesdames Dumont and Jaffronelli, each fanning themselves with a programme. I recognized some of the other audience faces as vaguely familiar from bingo night, but many seemed young to middle-aged and new to me. Family members of the kids in the play I figured. Occasionally, someone visited knitting lady and made a deposit to her cash box in exchange for something, but it was hard to make out what from this distance. Which had me wishing someone had trained a camera on her. After the quick vanishing act of the money at the tea reading, I was thinking her definition of treasurer may be a bit loose.

I was trying to get a better view of her table when a tall kid pushed past us to central backstage and burst out from the curtain to a round of applause and a few quiet laughs. I teetered on the chair and scrambled to withdraw the Bunny toes from the backrest slats so I could dismount without toppling over.

"*Voilà*." Camille adjusted my Bunny ears. "This is it. The last scene before you go on. We need to get you to your entrance position."

And with that, Laurent disappeared, presumably to get in his own position for filming.

I shuffled along with Camille as she steered me behind the curtain to the center spot the tall kid had just vacated. A hum of music soared and I froze. Camille assured me she wouldn't leave for the closet until my show was done and the money was dropped. Then she urged me forward through the curtain where I found myself standing center stage amidst the fake trees, a narrow spotlight hitting my face. Nothing hid me from the audience. No kids and no long dining table. The table had been split apart into two short ones, turned sideways, and set to the stage sides. The kids gathered, humming like a swarm of bees, in clustered circles at the head of each table, topping them like dots of exclamation marks.

Slow rhythmic clapping beat from the audience.

"*Allez, allez. Danse!*" Camille whispered to me.

I blinked at the light in my eyes and began shimmying the Bunny feet. Then the light blurred as the throng of kids rushed at me and my feet shimmying turned to outright jogging, slipping and sliding in the clunky yeti paws. Around the trees, by the table, in wild zigzags. Anywhere to get away from the pack of kids. Pretend chase my patootie! These kids were moving at full tilt! Beads of sweat from my upper lip trickled into my mouth, salty and dampening the lining of the Bunny head, heightening its acrid smell.

"Hum! Hum!" I heard coming from somewhere. Camille, probably, from behind the curtain, reminding me about the song. But I was too busy running to hum. And for the life of me I couldn't remember the tune of Frère Jacques even though I was sure the kids were humming a tune close to it, bits of it drowned out by the drumming that had returned to my ears.

"Drop it. Drop it now!" I heard Camille say as I ran by the curtain, two kids clutching my legs.

I retrieved the money bundle I'd tucked into a small panel I'd discovered at the base of the rounded Bunny tummy, and I let the bundle drop as I shook one kid free of my leg and scratched at my other leg to dislodge the second kid, veering off just short of crashing the both of us into a table as I headed for the black spot of paint on the floor for a reprieve.

Three kids blocked the spot, so I feigned throwing chocolate eggs across the stage in the hopes of distracting at least one of them, lucking out when two lost focus and I was able to skip by and land in the black area, one giant Bunny foot hitting first and plunging through the dark circle that swallowed me up whole, the stage disappearing from view as I plummeted to the depths below.

13

---

*P*LOOP! I LANDED, butt first on something squishy that released a cloud of dust like chalk mist. I tasted the dust more than saw it. The Bunny head twisting in my fall, leaving me limited vision but allowing dust particles to seep in and settle on my face like grainy fog, itching my eyes and tickling my nose.

"Achoo! Aaachoo!"

A sneeze sounded with enough force to blow the Bunny head off. If the sneeze had come from me, that is.

"Achooo!"

It went again. This time followed by a hiccup.

I pulled at the Bunny head with my paws, tugging at it to come off, so I could get my full bearings, but all it would do is swivel. I rotated it until I could see out the eyeholes, and a man's hand and lower body came into view. The hand held a screwdriver pointed at me. Beyond him near darkness.

From somewhere to my right I heard a gurgle of male words slurred together in French and the sharp sound of shattering glass.

I yanked harder on the Bunny head. This was no time to have tunnel vision even if it was dual tunnel vision. Not with screwdrivers coming at me and broken glass in the vicinity.

Another hand became visible, different skin tone, more olive, and reached towards me. On reflex, I flinched and reeled rearward, toppling fanny over teakettle style in an awkward backwards summersault, my feet hitting the dismount like a rusty gymnast.

A new hiccup went off somewhere to my left, and I grabbed the Bunny ears with both paws and pulled with all my might. With a "crreech" the Bunny head finally came off, sending me back a step, crashing into a cement wall. A cloud of dust followed me, landing and sticking to the Bunny suit like craft glitter.

My nose tingled and a series of tiny sneezes rushed out. Out of nowhere, a tissue pushed at my face and I smacked it away. Normally I had much better manners, but I was acting more on raw instinct than on decorum. Given the circumstances, I think even Miss Manners would give me a pass on my behavior. I was still trying to make sense of my surroundings and the screwdriver thing. Not to mention my fall from on high. That was no painted-on hole that swallowed me up. It was real. And how it got that way was likely no mistake.

The lighting notched up and the tissue came at me again, gentler this time. And I saw past it to the owner of the hand extending it. Wiry guy aka Broomman aka Monsieur Jaffronelli.

I hesitated before accepting the tissue as I took in the space around me in the brighter light. A basement by the looks of it. Unfinished, mechanical gizmos ticking and tapping away in the corner, open toolbox nearby, large grey carpet remnant in the middle set with two battered recliners with picnic coolers as side tables, a battered standing lamp, and a giant pouffe. The pouffe soft and squishy, dust mites dancing above in the light glow. My landing strip no doubt.

Another hiccup went, and I followed the sound to find Broomman's buddy Rakeman aka Monsieur Dumont to my side. He leaned into me, poking his screwdriver in the air less than a foot from my chin.

"*Regarde*, Alexandro," he said. "It's the little rabbit." His mouth creased into a twitchy smile, his upper lip peaking and dropping, peaking and dropping. Reminding me of his eyebrow wave the first time I'd seen him. His hand rose and fell along with his mouth, jittery and jabbing the screwdriver forward and backwards, the tip nearly grazing my skin.

I could feel the hard cement of the wall at my back, holding me in place. Smell the fumes from his mouth, 100% proof if I had to guess. With a hint of fruit.

Prickly heat crept up my confined spine. The jabbing screwdriver in my face and 100% proof were not a good combination.

Monsieur Dumont coughed up another hiccup and Monsieur Jaffronelli laughed, rocked back on his heels, and pointed at him. "Hah, you lose again! You said rabbit!"

Monsieur Dumont paused, confusion flickering on his face and disappearing when he raised a bottle to his mouth, tipped his head back, and drank.

I watched, baffled, no doubt confusion creeping onto my face, too.

"*Et alors*, what's going on down there?"

The question came from above, and I looked up to see Camille's face peering down from a hole in the ceiling. Before I could think of a reply, her face was replaced by men's shoes followed by black jean-clad legs dropping down and Laurent landing behind Monsieur Dumont, who flinched and sloshed crimson liquid on his shirtfront.

A minute later, Camille landed near Monsieur Jaffronelli. She scanned the scene and asked again what was going on.

Laurent said nothing and eased the screwdriver out of Monsieur Dumont's hand. Laurent wasn't waiting for answers to any questions. Probably Laurent's training was to disarm and de-escalate tension and ask questions later. Even if that disarming amounted to disavowing an old man of a screwdriver. Laurent didn't like to take chances when it came to potential weapons in dubious situations. And someone waving around a sharp tool in close quarters would definitely qualify as a potential hazard in Laurent's book.

Laurent's attention then settled on me, moving from my paws to my eyes and back again.

I looked at the tissue clasped in one paw and realized it wasn't alone. It had a companion. One Bunny ear. The other ear still attached to the head now tucked under my arm, deflated, threads streaming from a torn seam. The result of freeing myself from the Bunny head.

Laurent said nothing in words, but his eyes were not happy to see the torn ear.

I knew exactly where his mind was going, and I shook my head, letting him know the ear wasn't collateral damage in any kind of physical scuffle.

Laurent's eyes didn't lose much of their "not happy" vibe, so I stuffed the torn-off Bunny ear into the tummy pouch where I'd hid the money bundle earlier, going for an "out of sight out of mind" thing. My own twinge of guilt rising from ripping the costume even if it was accidental.

That left me still holding the tissue I'd gotten from Monsieur Jaffronelli. The tissue I saw on closer inspection was made of white cloth, like a hankie. Making it more personal and bringing an "ick" to mind at the thought of borrowing a hankie from a stranger. Especially since it also had a dark blotch at its border making it look used. Double ick. Although on second look, the blotch had form, less like dirt and more like an etching. Or an insignia. Like a monogram. The image reminding me of another swath of white cloth with a blotch near its edge. Two in fact.

Monsieur Jaffronelli's gaze met mine for an instant before moving skyward when a sudden roar of thunder shuddered from above. The thunder grew louder and the ceiling shook. Glances passed all around and everyone shifted to the edges of the room in unspoken unison. Like we were seeking safety in an earthquake or a hurricane.

From the hole in the ceiling, a burst of colored paper came raining down. We all stood in perplexed silence a beat, watching. The papers were rectangular and covered in various faces and numbers. They smelled of coated plastic and were accompanied by a billowing sheet of white fabric that I suspected had been tucked into my Bunny belly not long ago. The second money bundle wrapper. The kids must have torn it open thinking it was filled with Easter treats.

A twenty dollar bill landed by Camille's foot. She caught my eye and smiled. After all, it wasn't everyday money rained from on high.

Monsieur Dumont hiccupped, and Monsieur Jaffronelli grabbed the hankie in my hand, stuffed it into his pocket, and scurried to the far side of the room.

Shrieks of laughter and excitement rang out above as the thunderous thumps above slowed, and Julie's muffled voice calling for calm could be heard between children's cries amid a flutter of a few more bills wafting down.

From across the room, Monsieur Jaffronelli struggled with a doorknob, tugging at it. The door rattled, there was a scraping sound of metal, and his hand came away with a glass bulb as he stumbled back a few steps. He turned, glanced my way, and let out the mother of all sighs.

FEET POUNDED OUTSIDE the door and it flew open, Mesdames Dumont and Jaffronelli marching in. Adam and *tante* Claudette close behind.

"Lora!" Adam called to me, jogging the distance between us. "Thank goodness you're all right." He wrapped his arms around me and pulled me into a hug. "You disappeared and everyone laughed like it was part of the play, so I thought nothing of it at first. Then I saw Camille rush onstage and I knew something was up." He released the hug and gestured at Claudette. "Claudette showed me the way down as soon as we made our way through the crowd."

Monsieur Dumont brushed a few bills off a recliner, let out a high-pitched hiccup like a quack, then sat and took a swig from his bottle.

Monsieur Jaffronelli inched towards the other recliner, still clutching the doorknob, and lowered himself into the chair on a groan.

The church ladies huddled together by the doorway and scoped the room, from the money on the floor to the hole in the ceiling to the men. in the recliners. Then the trio turned tail to leave.

Laurent swung his eyes to me and shook his head. It was the hallway scene outside the church closet after the Bunny feet drop all over again.

Only this time *Les Femmes de l'Église* ladies weren't halted by Laurent's order to stop. This time Camille barred their way, filling the doorway and fixing them with a stare that could stop Niagara Falls mid stream.

The ladies sighed and pulled an about face towards the room, their gazes briefly skimming the men in the recliners before dispersing. Claudette's focus turned to the ceiling hole, Madame Jaffronell's focus went to her husband, and Madame Dumont fixated on the floor.

I'd noticed a whisper of a frown on Madame Dumont, her chin dipping some, but rather than the glaze her eyes had worn at the tea reading, they were subdued, almost sad.

Monsieur Dumont hiccupped again and pulled at the collar of his shirt. "*Mon Dieu il fait chaud ici.*" He looked at his hands, one holding tight to his bottle, the other empty, then pointed at me. "You, rabbit, what you do with my screwdriver?"

"Ah, ah, ah." Monsieur Jaffronelli wagged two fingers at Monsieur Dumont. "You did it again! You said rabbit."

Monsieur Dumont giggled and tipped his bottle to his mouth. Dribbles of red streams escaped his target and rolled onto his cheeks. He came up for air and reached to set the bottle on his cooler side-table, missing by about half a foot. His bottle fell to the ground, its impact quieted by the carpet developing damp spots near the bottleneck.

I bent to pick up the wine and place it on the makeshift side table. "It's okay, Monsieur Dumont," I said. "Your screwdriver is just fine." I gestured at Laurent to show Monsieur Dumont the screwdriver he'd confiscated.

Laurent held up the screwdriver and Monsieur Dumont squinted at it, moving his squint up to Laurent's face. "What are you waiting for, *mon gars*? If you have the screwdriver, go and fix the heat!" He pointed a bony finger at some ticking machines in the corner.

I skimmed over to Madame Dumont, her eyes still downcast, her cheeks growing pink. And probably not owing to the excess heat.

From her side, Claudette patted Madame Dumont's shoulder

but kept quiet. As did Madame Jaffronelli who cautiously picked her way over to her husband, avoiding as best she could the litter of money on the floor. Hard to do since she was clearly trying to simultaneously ignore it as though pretending it wasn't even there.

At the approach of his wife, Monsieur Jaffronelli smiled, and reached for her hand. "Ah, my angel."

She scowled at him and shook her head. "You old fool."

Monsieur Jaffronelli's smile grew into a full grin and he kissed the palm of his wife's hand. "Only a fool for you, Angel."

Camille's hands went to her hips and she rolled her eyes. "*Tout ca,*" she said, pausing to wave her hand in a large circle like a figurative net encasing the entirety before her, "*est complètement fou.* Does anyone have a clue what's going on?"

I heard a sharp inhale of breath and traced it to Madame Dumont. She pinched her lower lip in her teeth like it would retract the noise, and our eyes met. Not for long, but long enough to read the mix of anxiety and embarrassment she had brewing.

"We were, um, celebrating," I said, breaking from our eye-lock and moving closer to Monsieur Dumont's chair.

Camille arched her brow at me and Adam asked, "Celebrating what?"

I patted Monsieur Dumont on the shoulder and crossed the fingers inside the paw behind my back, crushing the Bunny head tighter to my body with my elbow in the process. "The success of our trick." I smiled wide. "These two nice men made a real hole in the stage for me to jump through. We thought it would make the play finale better. And it worked, right? Wasn't it a big surprise when I disappeared?"

Monsieur Dumont perked up and Monsieur Jaffronelli looked on with curiosity as I winked at him.

Laurent's lips twitched and he leaned against the wall. Camille rolled her eyes at me from the doorway where she remained planted. She knew, of course, that I was fibbing. The fib came to me when I noticed a circular piece of wood set by the toolbox in the corner. Which by the looks of it seemed to fit the stage hole, but I was guessing hadn't been cut out on Julie's or anybody's say-so, least of all mine. My guess was the hole had been made by accident. Some misguided interpretation probably by Monsieur Dumont who, if his proficiency with the heating system was any indication, was not the world's best custodian. At least not while he was in a "celebrating" state. And judging by what I'd witnessed, I was thinking that may be his state more often than not and probably I was looking at the sommelier of the church closet wine collection.

Madame Dumont looked at me, her face softening, the tiniest of smiles forming. Not big toothy grin style, more subtle, almost shy. Maybe even a hint of gratitude at my covering of what I suspected was her husband's drinking problem and likely something she had been probably grappling with for a while.

Camille grinned at me and swept an arm in the air. "And the money on the floor?"

She was playing now, egging me on. Probably she had no clue where my fib was coming from and was eager to hear what else I'd come up with. Only I had nothing.

I glanced from Laurent to Monsieur Jaffronelli. The hankies probably connected Monsieur Jaffronelli to the missing bingo money bundles, but if so I didn't know how or why. Or even if the money going missing was entirely a crime. After all, it was stored in the church closet. One could argue the money was moved not missing. If one were really motivated. Still, since I was the current suspect in what up until now had been considered a heist, it would be nice to out the real culprit. I really wanted to clear myself, but I was sensing there was more to the bingo pilfering than met the eye.

"Um…," I said then trailed off, nowhere to go with this one.

"That," Laurent said, moving from the wall to my side, stepping back a bit under the glare of his aunt but continuing to address the room, "is the test of Monsieur Jaffronelli. A surprise also. A new way for the Easter Bunny to pass chocolate eggs to the kids, inside bundles filled with candy the Bunny throws when she jumps in the hole. Then instead of chasing the Bunny for their treats, the kids can have fun collecting bundles and bursting them open after the Bunny leaves."

"Right," I agreed, catching on and continuing. "And all the kids could have baskets to collect the eggs in and the one who gets the most gets a big prize."

Adam surveyed the money on the ground. "And you're giving out money, too? That's a *really* big haul for a kid. There's got to be a few hundred dollars on the floor."

Claudette bustled forward and began gathering the money. "*Non, non.* The money is not for the kids."

"Uh, that's right," I said. "The money was just for the test. At the real play tomorrow the bundle will be filled with chocolate eggs. It was all Monsieur Jaffronelli's idea. He was afraid if the kids got their hands on too much candy now they'd eat themselves sick before performance time, so he just substituted the money for the rehearsal. He didn't think anyone would open the bundles at the rehearsal and just used something handy. I think that's bingo money, right Monsieur Jaffronelli? And it goes back to *Les Femmes de l'Église*, right?"

Monsieur Jaffronelli slid me a conspiratorial smile laced with indebtedness for not outing him for squirreling away the money in his hankies, and he nodded repeatedly, like a meme stuck on replay. "Sure, sure."

Camille had joined her aunt collecting bills from the floor and combined their piles. "*Alors là,*" she said, passing over the lot to

Madame Dumont. "Now you have some of your money, I'm sure the rest will come." She directed a near glare at Monsieur Jaffronelli "And everything is square with Lora, *n'est-ce-pas?*"

Now it was Madame Dumont's turn to nod. Curt and polite, earlier vulnerabilities subsiding, *Femmes de l'Église* group head stance returning. Like a veil had been momentarily lifted and was drawing closed.

"Here you all are!" Julie called, bustling into the room, popping chocolate hens like they were Tic Tacs." We've got a full blown anarchy on our hands upstairs. I could use some help with—" she froze midsentence, her eyes bugging out when she saw me. "Good grief! What did you do to the Bunny?"

All eyes turned to me, zeroing in on the Bunny head crushed under my arm, ear dangling, thread snaking down to the floor. Other ear poking out of my Bunny belly pocket.

I felt heat rush up my neck and the sting of Claudette's look of horror when she caught sight of the maimed Bunny costume.

Fabulous, just when I managed to get myself out of trouble with one church lady I was leaping into trouble with another. Lucky for me Claudette's tea reading talent didn't extend to mind reading or she'd have me on Lent breaking, too, because the thought of disappointing Claudette had me totally coveting Julie's chocolate hens.

14

"**Y**OU SURE YOU know what you're doing with that thing?" Adam asked me.

"It can't be that hard. I took a sewing class in eighth grade," I assured him. "I'm sure it's like riding a bike. It will come back to me."

We were home, in the dining room. Me hunched over an old sewing machine that had belonged to Adam's mom. Him watching from the sideboard. He had dirt stains on his sweatshirt and a nest of dust in his hair from unburying the machine from its sojourn in the basement.

"There," I said, straightening and seating myself. "See? I got all the wires attached and the needle threaded. The hard part's done." I picked up the Bunny head from the table and studied the pins I'd used to attach the torn ear into place.

Adam moved to the table. "It looks lopsided. You got one ear sticking to the top of the head and the other jutting out the side."

I held the face farther away from me. Adam was right. The torn ear was pinned too close to the side of the Bunny face.

I yanked out the pins and started over.

"My mom made a lot of my Halloween costumes when I was a kid," Adam said. "She used the machine for the main parts, but for a lot of the details like that she said it was better to sew them on by hand."

I glanced up, clenching the folded edge of fabric I was about to pin, and checked out the intact ear. Hmm. I couldn't tell if it had been stitched by hand or machine. I finished the pinning, placed the head on the dining table, and went to the kitchen.

"Mind if I use your laptop for a sec?" I said.

Adam followed me into the kitchen and over to the counter where he'd left his computer. "Be my guest. I'll just get it open for you." He tapped a key to revive his screen, put in his password, and pivoted the laptop my way. "You want to tell me why you're fixing this thing? And while you're at it, you want to explain that crazy after show in that basement with the loopy guys and the money on the floor?"

"I already told you on the way home. There was a mix-up with some missing money from a fundraising bingo and the money was found. That's all."

At least that was all I was telling Adam. Now that it was all over, I didn't see any reason to tell him about my stint as a suspect in a theft involving said missing money. The day he became a godfather was not also going to go down as the day his girlfriend dodged another sketchy situation. At least not if I could help it.

Adam eyed me, skeptical. Not buying my condensed version of the story.

I put my attention on the computer and pulled up a search engine.

"How to sew a bunny costume? Really, Lora?" Adam laughed, reading over my shoulder. "That's what you're searching? Why not: How to repair ears on a bunny costume I hate and am wearing anyway in a play I don't want to be in?"

I shot him a grimace and focused on my search returns. I scrolled down and clicked on a link that promised easy-sew instructions for beginners. As the page loaded, the doorbell rang and Adam went to answer it.

I blew out a sigh when the page of instructions came in. It was for a kid's one-piece rabbit costume that looked more gingerbread man with big ears than bunny.

"*Mais alors*, I didn't know you could sew," Camille said, coming into the kitchen via the dining room route and doing a double-take to the machine set up on the table.

"I'm beginning to think I can't," I told her. "But I've got to fix the Bunny ear."

"You hate that rabbit suit."

"Yes, but your aunt Claudette loves it. She thinks it's really cute."

Camille shrugged. "Then let her fix it. She has a sewing room at home. In five minutes she could fix the ear." Camille grabbed for one of the chocolate bunny suckers on a stick Adam had got at a local store earlier in the week and set in a mug on the counter. She had the cellophane wrapper halfway off when she crimped it back in place and returned it to the mug.

"Not this again," I said. "Eat the darn chocolate already! It doesn't bother me."

Adam slowed his re-entry into the kitchen from answering the door to Camille. "Sounds like you two could use a little girl time." He reached for his laptop. "If you're finished with this, I'll just take it upstairs. I've got a few emails to return."

Was I finished with my computer search? I wasn't sure. Not that it mattered since Adam was already on his way to his home office, his laptop tucked under his arm.

"*Mais alors,*" Camille said. "That was some show you put on at rehearsal."

She'd moved from the counter to the fridge where she was partially hidden by the door as she scanned the contents inside in grazing mode.

"I know," I said. "I totally messed up the dancing and humming. But those kids were fierce. I didn't expect them to run after me like that so quickly."

Camille let the fridge door close and came back into view. "Not that show. The one after in the room under the stage. With your stories about the 'celebrating' and Monsieur Jaffronelli testing the bundle for distributing *les chocolats* for the kids."

A flush came to my cheeks. "I'll cop to the 'celebrating' thing, but the bundle story was all Laurent."

Camille rolled her eyes at me. "It was you who said the money for the test came from the bingos, no? And that Monsieur Jaffronelli was returning it there?"

"Well, yeah."

"*Alors voilà,* that makes it your story, too." She drummed her fingers on the counter. "So how did you know it was Monsieur Jaffronelli who took the money?"

I explained about the hankies with their monograms like dirt smudges.

"Ah. Good catch. And you covered for him why?"

I shrugged. "Monsieur Jaffronelli's not a bad guy. I get the feeling if he took the money it was for a good reason, or at least one he should tell his wife about in private before confessing to a committee of onlookers."

"Very generous considering you were the one accused of the crime."

"I don't think Monsieur Jaffronelli knew that. His wife told me she didn't believe I had anything to do with it, so I'm guessing she never mentioned my part to her husband. I'm sure if he'd known Madame Dumont wanted to report me to the police, he would have confessed."

"He did, sort of, after you left. He said he was afraid his wife's fundraising was too good and would win her the head of the *Femmes de L'Église* role in the new election, so he skimmed a little off the profits and 'moved' them, planning to give everything back after the elections."

"You mean he did it to sabotage his own wife?"

"He didn't want her to win and be in the movie with Monsieur Ménard. He thought Ménard had his eye on his wife."

I smiled. "Ah, that's kinda sweet if you think about it. Still jealous after all those years together. I mean, it's crummy that he'd undermine his wife like that, but his reason was sweet and it's not like he took the money for himself."

"*Ça c'est vrai.* He hid it in the closet. Only his sommelier friend found a couple of the bundles and Jaffronelli had to pay him off to keep him quiet."

My mind flashed to the tickets I'd seen Monsieur Jaffronelli pass to Monsieur Dumont in the parking lot. Must have been the payoff.

"Well, at least now they can get on with their church group leader elections on even footing and nobody's blaming me anymore."

"True. And Madame Dumont is impressed with you again after you covered her husband's 'happy' state with the 'celebrating' thing." Camille crooked an eyebrow at me. "Interesting choice that. Covering for the sommelier, too?"

"I had to. Madame Dumont looked so sad about his drinking. And embarrassed like she didn't want people to know."

Camille nodded. "Seems you're not alone in that feeling. After you left the rehearsal, *ma tante* confided to me that Monsieur

Dumont has been drinking for years and all the *Femmes de l'Église* ladies knew, but they pretended not to out of respect for Madame Dumont. That's why they tried to bolt when you dropped the wine from the Bunny feet outside the church closet."

"Oh, right, of course." I thought about their reaction when they came across Laurent and me in the church hallway and they tried to flee. "So their response was about the wine and had nothing to do with the bundle of money."

Camille shook her head. "They didn't even know what the bundle was until Laurent opened it. But they knew Monsieur Dumont hid wine in the closet. Everyone knew but the priest. They were afraid now the secret would come out and Monsieur Dumont would get fired. He's not old enough to retire, but he's too old to get another job."

I nodded understanding. "I get it. The three *Mumketeers* went super quiet when Laurent questioned them to avoid talking about Monsieur Dumont."

"They're honest ladies. It's one thing to pretend not to know anything to spare someone's feelings, it's another to lie under direct questions. Better to stay quiet." Camille poked her head in the cookie jar on the counter and wrinkled her nose.

I grabbed a plate, stuck my hand in the jar, and brought out a chocolate chip muffin. "Take it already," I said. "If it makes you feel better, I won't even look at you while you eat." I moved into the dining room and busied myself with having another go at ear pinning. "And not to burst your story or anything, but the ladies did lie. They said they knew nothing about the wine. Or the money. Plus, they then accused me of taking the money."

"According to them, Laurent never asked if they knew who the wine belonged to specifically. So they didn't have to lie, only side-step the question. The money was a different thing. That, they were surprised about."

"And suspicious," I said. "Don't forget suspicious. So suspicious they were ready to blame *me*."

Camille wandered in from the kitchen sans plate, a glass of water in her hand. "I don't think any of them really suspected you. But they knew someone had to have put the money in the closet and until they knew who, better to spread around possibilities than to have all the scrutiny on Monsieur Dumont as the custodian. And better to get everyone to focus on the money and forget about the wine."

Hmm. So Laurent was right. Accusing me was partially a diversion tactic. Not to divert from the real thief so much as to keep focus off of the wine and any possible association to Monsieur Dumont. Suggesting I may be the culprit wasn't so much Madame Dumont distrusting me, it was her protecting her husband. Although to be fair, she really didn't know who took the money and I was probably as good a guess as any.

"I get the logic," I said, "but it wouldn't have been a great comfort if Madame Dumont had reported me to the police."

"*Non, non.* After the tea reading, she wouldn't have. The tea reading said you were free of any guilt so she knew you were not the thief."

"Is that what the whole "nothing" thing meant? In that case, everyone was clear of guilt, not just me. But seriously, they were going to take a tea reading as proof?"

"They're very spiritual. They believe tea readings are like spirits talking to them." Camille dragged out the chair across from me and seated herself. "Anyway, the tea reading was right. Nobody there did take the money."

That was true since the tea reading was over by the time the Monsieurs Dumont and Jaffronelli arrived. "Well, at least now that everything's out in the open maybe Monsieur Dumont can get some counseling for his addiction."

Camille nodded. "Maybe."

"It will be good for Madame Dumont, too. She'll be able to talk about it more with her friends and get real support, not just the silent type." My Bunny ear pinning complete, I flicked on the sewing machine and positioned my foot over the pedal, then paused. "But wait, none of that explains who locked me in the closet. You didn't also happen to find that out after Adam and I left, did you?"

Camille tapped the table. "*Oui, oui.* I almost forgot. That was Monsieur Dumont. And it was an accident. He saw the closet was unlocked and he bolted it thinking he'd forgotten to shut it after his last visit for a nip from his stash."

Hmm. Not sure I was buying that story. "What about when I was yelling inside to get out? He just left me there. That was no accident."

"He thought he was hearing voices. He didn't believe his ears. It happens sometimes he hears things when he's had too many nips."

I had the fabric in place and stomped on the sewing machine pedal, and a throbbing grind pierced the air.

Camille shot out of her seat. "*Mon Dieu, arrête, arrête!* You're killing it!"

I lifted my foot and bent for a closer look. "It looks fine. Let me try again. It's probably just because the machine hasn't been used in a long time. Probably it just needs to warm up or something."

I pressed on the peddle again, slower this time. The machine groaned a second then the fabric moved along the track. I smiled. That was better. I could so do this. I angled the needle point along as I removed pins, stopping once I'd made a full circle at the ear base and raised the needle lock. "And *voilà*," I exclaimed, sweeping the fabric out and into the air, the ear dropping to the floor, nothing but Bunny face left in my hand.

Pong sprang out from beneath the coffee table in the adjoining living room, snatched the ear, and ran off.

I ran after the dog and snatched the ear back before any stuffing could fall out.

"I don't get it," I said studying the machine. "It worked fine that time." I checked the thread spool. "And there's plenty of thread."

Camille had come around the table and was looking the machine over.

"*Mais voyons*, Lora. There's no thread in the bobbin."

"Bobbin?" Dang. I'd forgotten all about the bobbin when I'd set up the machine.

I heaved a big sigh and slumped into my chair.

Camille sighed, too. "Shove over," she said, practically bumping me out of my chair. "I'll do it."

Within minutes, Camille had the machine whirring and the Bunny ear attached. It was a bit crooked without benefit of a good pin line but attached.

"I thought you didn't know how to do crafty things like sewing," I said.

"Tell anyone and our friendship is over."

I grinned. "No worries. Your secret is safe with me."

Seemed like a lot of secrets were coming to light today. Except maybe the one I really wanted to know. The reason for *tante* Claudette's finger wag with Laurent. Of course that secret had nothing to do with me and it wasn't my place to ask about it, so I was guessing that would be the one secret that remained kept.

15

THE PLAY WAS scheduled for three in the afternoon. Right after she fixed the Bunny ear, Camille had taught me the song I was supposed to sing. I'd practiced the song and my two lines well into the evening and awoken in a sweat at six a.m. from a dream where I not only forgot the song and my lines during the performance, but the kids chased me out of the Bunny suit.

Sheesh, was I suggestive. Somehow I'd mingled my own performance anxiety with the fate of last year's Bunny and scared myself silly. I was way beyond performance anxiety by the time I pulled into the parking lot outside the bingo hall/play venue. I was harboring a full-blown anxiety attack. Not only would I humiliate myself if I screwed this up, but I'd ruin the kids' play. Even worse, I'd embarrass Claudette and she'd be sorry she ever picked me to play Easter Bunny for her group.

"Breathe," I told myself in a soothing tone. "Breathe." I tried to remember a yoga breathing exercise I'd learned that pulled air in through the nose deep into the stomach then out through the mouth. Or was it in through the mouth, out through the nose?

I tried both and decided the first felt better so kept that up for five breaths, eyes closed, hands resting on my thighs behind the steering wheel. By the last round, my heart rate felt nearly normal and my limbs lost most of their rigid tension.

Slowly, I opened my eyes on the final exhale, the last whoosh of air catching when Laurent came into view across the lot. He was wearing jeans and a tailored jacket, and his hair was billowing in the breeze. Beside him was *tante* Claudette and her wagging finger. Only this time, her other hand extended and dropped something in Laurent's upturned palm.

I stretched across to the glove compartment, whipped it open, and extracted a set of opera glasses I'd recently stashed in there after repeated reminders from Camille about the importance of PIs carrying binoculars for stakeouts and emergency snooping.

I fixed the opera glasses on Laurent's hand. Whatever Claudette had placed there had his fingers clenched over it, hidden from view. I sighed. Not so much about missing out on seeing anything, more about the realization that my curiosity may be getting a tad out of hand, as it were. I didn't used to be the nosy type. Probably it was the PI job notching up my curious side.

Claudette's head pivoted my way and I whisked the glasses aside, knocking the water canister askew in the cup holder by my seat. I righted myself and offered Claudette a finger wave. She waved back, her chignon hairdo unraveling around her ears from the swift spring wind the day had brought with it along with a few clouds and an unseasonable chill. She hugged her sweater to herself, bowed her head to the wind, and hurried to the building entrance. She turned back at the door and motioned to Laurent to join her, and with a side glance at me accompanied by a slight nod and smile, he followed in Claudette's tracks.

"What are you doing in there?" I heard someone ask, the voice muffled by the closed window and the wind, making the words sound almost like they had come from some omnipotent source in the ether.

My face flushed and my hand flew to my chest, sure I was being busted for my voyeur moment with the opera glasses.

I scoped my surrounding and saw my questioner was Camille, talking to me from one car over. Instantly, the heat in my cheeks mellowed with relief. At least my spying hadn't been witnessed by an omnipotent being. Or a stranger.

Camille's parking spot was empty when I pulled in and somehow I'd missed her arrival. Probably because I'd been too busy spying.

I returned the glasses to the glove box and grabbed my purse. By the time I got out of my Mini, Camille was out of her car and making her way over to me.

"It happened again," I told her.

"*Quoi?*"

"Your aunt Claudette's finger wag at Laurent." I moved to collect the Bunny suit from the back seat. "I really wish I knew what it was about." I knew immediately after I said it I was just feeding my curious side, but I couldn't help myself.

Camille eyed me but stayed quiet.

I folded the costume over my forearm and locked my car. "Except this time she gave him something, but I couldn't see what it was. Did you ever find out what the finger wag was about?"

She shrugged. "I forgot about it. *Mais*, if you want to know so much just ask Laurent."

"I can't ask Laurent. It's none of my business. Plus, it could be personal. I don't want to ask if it's personal." Truth be told, the more personal it was, the more I wanted to know. But wanting to know and asking were two different things. I'd lock my lips before I'd ask Laurent or Claudette.

Camille grinned. "You won't ask, but you'll spy? *Très intéressant.*"

"I blame you," I said as we walked across the lot to go into the building. "It was you who made me buy those mini binoculars. I wouldn't even have been able to spy if it wasn't for you."

"Those are for work," she reminded me. "What you do with them when you're not working is all on you." She laughed but stopped talking as we got inside and wound our way through clusters of early-bird playgoers milling about inside.

Halfway through the room, one of the playgoers waylaid Camille. I paused then continued on without her when it seemed she may be waylaid for a while.

I got to the makeshift backstage and looked for a place to get into the Bunny costume, happy to find an unoccupied chair in the corner where I could unload my jacket and skirt. I positioned a nearby clothes rack in front of the chair like a screen for a bit of privacy. Below the skirt, I'd worn leggings with a long-sleeve shirt on top that I planned to wear under the Bunny suit, so full privacy wasn't an issue for my costume change. The privacy was more about shielding me from embarrassment. The shaggy carpet suit with yeti feet sporting stick toes was not helped by crooked ears. The less I was seen in the get-up in public the better.

I hooked the suit on the end of the clothes rack and turned to the chair to shed my skirt and jacket. When I turned back, the Bunny suit was gone.

In its place was a hanger draped in a white and pink velour number, a small bag looped onto it at the top. I peered around the clothes stand. Nobody loitered, just some kids practicing lines and a couple others sitting on the floor playing video games on hand-held devices. The only grownups in view were parents wrangling costumes on younger children.

I unhooked the bag, looked inside, and pulled out a set of bunny ears. Pristine white and secured to a headband, cute pink lining the inner ear. I stuck my hand in the bag again and found a makeup kit and a note. I unfolded the note. It read: *Nobody puts mon petit lapin in old carpets. Or hides her eyes in a furry head. Try this instead. Ears and whiskers included.* It was signed with a big L but didn't need to be. Only one person called me his *petit lapin.*

I smiled and slid on the new suit. It had a side zipper, and the velour was fur thick and lined in a stretchy cotton. Nothing like the loopy shag carpet. The paws were a thinner velour with sticky patches below like yoga socks. Not a stick toe in sight.

The makeup kit included a small mirror and instructions for creating the perfect bunny nose, cheeks, and eyes. I fixed my face and finished the look by retying my pony tail and adding the ears.

When the play had started and most of the kids were onstage, I toddled over to the full-length mirror to take in the whole ensemble and grinned at my reflection. All Easter Bunny. Not even a faint hint of yeti.

I moved to my entrance point where Julie passed me a basket of chocolate eggs covered in brightly-colored foil wrappers and assured me the hole in the stage had been fixed and was ready for my finale.

As I waited for my cue, I tested the sticky pads on the soles of the Bunny feet for slip resistance. Perfect.

I gave a silent "thank you" to Laurent, wiggled the feet, and winked at Julie. "Just let the kids try to catch me in these babies."

16

"*I*'M THINKING YOUR aunt needs a revolving front door," I whispered to Camille. "She's got more visitors coming through than the ladies' room at the theatre during inter- mission."

Camille nodded and shuffled me closer to Claudette's living room fireplace where I eyed the mantel. After the play, Claudette announced a gathering at her house to mark the end of Lent, and she'd been so pleased with my Easter Bunny performance she'd invited me to come along. Since we'd arrived, I noticed the mantel adornments were minus a few cookie boxes and comic books.

I shifted my eyes to the doorway as more of Camille's family members stuffed themselves into the room.

"Is Puddles coming?" I asked Camille, referring to the guy she "unofficially" lived with.

Camille shook her head. "He's with Lucia. Her church also breaks Lent tonight. He doesn't follow Lent, but he's going anyway to be with her."

I smiled. Lucia was Puddles' daughter and I'd played a small role in reuniting them after years apart. Knowing they got to share holidays together again was heartwarming.

"What about Adam?" Camille asked me. "He's not with you?"

"He's coming in a bit. He texted me that he had one last errand to do for Tina before the little family went home and he'd be all mine for the weekend."

A small hand snaked behind Camille and me and snagged a bag of chips off the mantel. The hand's owner clutched the bag to her little chest and made a dash for the basement door. A few more kids claimed their offerings and followed suit.

I smiled at Camille. "Gee, you better hurry and recoup your peanut butter before someone runs off with it. Now that Lent's over, you don't want to deprive yourself. Help me cut a path out and I'll fetch you a spoon from the kitchen so you can dig in."

Camille rolled her eyes at me. "If someone wants the peanut butter, they can have it. Anyway, only the kids can take their offerings now. The rest of us have to wait until *tante* Claudette does the official closing of Lent. It's tradition."

A teenage girl nodded at Camille in passing as she pulled a card from the mantel. The card had a picture of an ice cream container.

"Wow," I said to Camille when the girl headed for the basement. "Ice cream. That's a big sacrifice. I don't know if I could do ice cream." Truth be told I was having a hard enough time not snatching my chocolate back even after hearing Camille's news about grownups having to wait for the traditional Lent closing time.

"That's Vicky," Camille said. "Vicky's allergic to dairy. She eats that soy ice cream. The picture on her card was for dairy ice cream."

"Ah, so Vicky's caught on to the nuanced fake offering thing already. And the card?"

"Cards are allowed. They're better for perishable things or

symbols of habits. Two years ago, one of my cousins gave up swearing. You should have seen his card. *Ma tante* put it in an envelope so the kids wouldn't read it."

A family of five entered the living room and the three kids pushed their way over to the mantel, the littlest one dragging a footstool over and climbing atop to reach for a box of Lego. He pulled it out Jenga style from the bottom of a stack of other boxes that dropped down in a neat pile, reducing the stack by one.

I watched the kids run for the basement as Camille introduced me to the kids' parents and several other incoming family members. With the house abuzz with cousins and chatter, I almost missed Adam among the crowd, trying to make his way over to me.

When we connected, he passed me a bouquet of slightly squished flowers and pecked my cheek. "Great performance, hon. Sorry I missed the end with your song but your dance was really good."

"*Oui*," one of Camille's cousins agreed. "You should be the Easter Bunny every year."

"And that costume," another cousin said. "Way better than that old one they used to have. That thing was so old, I think it was around when I was a kid." He laughed, the laugh turning to a cough when Claudette appeared through the parted crowd and everyone fell silent.

Behind Claudette, I caught sight of Laurent leaning against the archway between the living room and the foyer.

He tipped his chin in my direction when our eyes met, making me wonder if he'd heard his cousins' comments. Normally, in a room full of people chattering I wouldn't think so, but with Laurent anything was possible. He could pick up on sounds like bloodhounds picked up on scents.

I had yet to thank Laurent for the costume upgrade and tried to mouth him a "thank you" that got lost in transmission, blocked from view by the Lego kid, returned from the basement and circling a small plane in the air, miraculously already transformed from fragments to full form.

Then Claudette began speaking in French, addressing the room, pausing here and there with the occasional tapping near her collarbone for emotional emphasis. Most of her words were above my translation pay grade, but I caught the drift of her speech. If Lent was an Olympic sport, this would be closing ceremonies material.

When she was done, general chit chat resumed and Claudette pulled me aside and presented me with a gift box. A small token she said for helping with the kids' pageant.

I tucked Adam's flowers in the crook of my arm as she came in close for a hug. She placed the present in my free hand, whispering her admiration for how I'd handled things with her *Femmes de l'Église* group and the little matter of the bingo money, and finished our embrace with cheek kisses.

I blinked to hold in the tears stinging my eyes at her words of appreciation, and she gave my upper arm a light squeeze, reminding me of something my mother may have done.

I assured Claudette a present was completely unnecessary and that I was happy to help.

Claudette glanced over her shoulder and patted the little box she'd given me. "Open it only when you're alone, *ma belle*." Then she wagged her finger at me, like a pre-emptive warning, dare I not follow her instructions, and she trundled off.

"*Alors*, what did *you* do?" Camille asked, moving in beside me, playful lilt in her voice.

"Excuse me?"

"The finger wag?"

"Oh, that. Nothing." I jostled the little box I got from Claudette.

"Your aunt was just passing me this gift for helping with the play, and she was telling me to open it later alone. The finger wag was for emphasis I think."

Camille crunched on a cracker, in think mode, but said nothing.

"Where'd you get the cracker?" I said.

She hooked a finger towards the doorway. "Kitchen. There's a buffet in there now that Lent's officially over. People are stocking up before the fast begins. Adam and I went in while you were talking with *tante* Claudette. Adam's still there. He got cornered by a couple of cousins in the market for new boyfriends. He's the only guy here they're not related to and they're vying for him. He'll be stuck there until they realize he's here with you."

She glanced about the room, only stragglers remaining. "But not to worry," she told me. "We can go soon."

My eyes drifted to the fireplace mantel. The jetsam on top had completely thinned out since the last time I'd checked, Camille's peanut butter jar prominently dominating the scanty remains. My chocolate wrapper barely visible, laying flat and marooned near the end.

"Gee, things really clear out fast. Is that it?" I said.

"What else would there be? After *tante* Claudette gives her closing speech, we all go. There's the fast on Friday and more gatherings on Sunday, but in smaller groups. This is the biggest gathering and even this is not everybody. This is more for the families with kids and to collect the Lent offerings."

I nodded. Camille had a huge family. No way everyone would fit in Claudette's little bungalow all at once. I hadn't even seen Camille's parents in attendance and Claudette's own daughter, Arielle, was still on vacation for the week somewhere hot and sunny with her beau, Jason.

"*Allez.*" Camille poked the gift box in my hand. "Open it already."

"I can't." I jostled the bouquet Adam had given me that filled the crook of my arm. "I don't have any hands left. Besides, I'm supposed to wait to open it until I'm alone."

Camille arched a brow. No sarcasm in her baby browns, just intrigue. She took the flowers from me and stuffed them, cellophane-wrapped stems and all, into the vase with the Easter lilies on the mantel.

"Hey," I said. "Careful. You're squishing the petals." I was mostly thinking about Adam's flowers, but Claudette's lilies weren't faring much better. "And your aunt won't be happy with you if she sees you messing with her Easter flowers."

"*Ma tante* won't notice a thing. She's busy with Laurent."

I followed Camille's gaze to the foyer where Claudette and Laurent were indeed in deep conversation. Serious looking faces but no finger wagging. Instead, a small box passed between them. A small box very similar to the one Claudette had given me.

I scanned the room, checking for more boxes in hands but didn't spot a thing.

Curious now, I moved to stand behind an armchair to block my hands from view and carefully slid the ribbon off the box and lifted the lid. Inside, nestled on spun cotton, was a small card, blue flowery teapot on the cover. I flipped it open. Printed on the right side were French words. Something about tea. Handwritten on the left was yesterday's date titling a list written in English. Not numbered but clearly demarked, item to item, syntax off but spelling spot on. From top to bottom it read: *Big changes coming; Old connections appear have caution; Soulmate soon in this room.* The last line was underlined. Three times.

I heard air blow by my ear when Camille let out a soft laugh as she read over my shoulder. "*Encore* the tea reading predictions!"

She plucked the card from my hands, examined it closer, and returned it to its box. "I love her to death but *ma tante* will never change. Isn't that the same predictions you got last time?"

I nodded. "Mostly." The bit in the middle was new and there was more info about a soulmate, but Camille was right about the rest. If the list hadn't included yesterday's date of the tea reading in the church kitchen, I might have taken it for the tea reading I'd had over the winter. My first with Claudette and another I'd been volunteered for by a Caron sib. That time Camille.

I looked over at the sib who'd volunteered me this time. Laurent, also peering at a card with a teapot on the front, the space between us unpopulated, his aunt no longer in sight.

Laurent's eyes stayed steady on his card before he closed it, slid it into his back pocket, and glanced my way.

I had the urge to rush over and compare cards. The urge dulling when Adam strolled in from the kitchen with Camille's young cousin flying his Lego plane between them. The cousin then ran to Camille to enlist her to join them and watch him fly it back to the kitchen.

"*Soulmate soon in this room.*" Underlined three times. The words flashed in my mind in neon lights, like a marquis. Blinking and bright against a night sky.

Did the card mean Adam? He was the first to enter the room, after all. Well, Adam and the little plane boy. But the plane boy didn't count. It would be at least twenty years before he'd be looking for a mate.

At my first tea reading, Claudette implied Adam wasn't my soulmate, so maybe this was her way of correcting that prediction.

I shut the lid on the card, resealed the box with the ribbon, and chuckled at myself. Was I really buying into Claudette's divinations? I mean, if Adam and I were meant to be together wasn't it because we made a good fit and not because of a bunch of soggy tea leaves. The whole idea that tea leaves could predict the future was crazy. And believing in said predictions had to be even crazier, right? Dangerous even. A gal could get into a whole heap of trouble leaving her destiny to some airy fairy fortune telling. Even if Claudette had got a few things right before. That was probably coincidence, not providence.

Plus, if I was going to believe one of Claudette's predictions I'd have to believe them all. I'd constantly be looking over my shoulder on the lookout for the big changes and the old connections thing. Way too time consuming and crazy making. I had to get a grip.

Look at Laurent, I told myself. He wasn't wasting time fixating on his card of predictions. He'd already slipped his destiny into his pocket, tucked away out of sight out of mind. He was over by the mantel now, snatching a tiny envelope from behind a leftover bag of corn chips. He paused at my chocolate wrapper, picked it up, and tossed it to me.

I hurried to catch the chocolate but didn't miss Laurent adding the envelope he'd snatched to the same pocket he'd placed his predictions. Probably the envelope contained his Lent offering. Which meant his offering fit on a card like the teenager with the ice cream pic. Yet, it was sealed away like the cousin with the swearing habit. Which didn't make sense. Laurent didn't swear much. As far as I knew, Laurent didn't have any habits to give up. Although there were a few things he did *I* wouldn't mind if he gave up. Like refusing to tell me what he *had* given up for Lent.

"*Alors*, let's go," Camille said, joining me again as Laurent was hailed to the hall by some cousin, and I missed my chance to ask him about the card or give him a proper thank you for the Bunny suit switch.

Camille grabbed her peanut butter and I motioned to the tub. "I thought you were leaving the peanut butter?"

"Food bank," she said, patting the jar. "*Et toi?* You got your chocolate?"

"Yup. Laurent just passed it to me."

"*Ah oui.* Laurent. I heard in the kitchen about his finger wag. You still want to know what it was about?"

"Of course I want to know! Do you even have to ask?"

Camille wiggled her fingers at my chocolate, and I broke a row off for her. If she wanted a payoff for the finger wag intel I was happy to oblige.

She grinned and accepted my offering while I indulged in a piece, too. "*Merci,* but I meant that's what the finger wag was about."

"Chocolate?"

"*Non, non.* Not chocolate. Lent. It seems *ma tante* thought Laurent cheated on his Lent commitment."

My heart did a double beat. "Laurent doesn't cheat. Laurent always follows the rules." Well, almost always. There was the little matter of him giving me the puppet doll. "Anyway, how would Claudette know?" I leaned in close to Camille and lowered my voice. "What was he supposed to give up?"

Camille waved her arm in the air. "Nobody knows except *tante* Claudette. And they made up about it, so it doesn't matter anymore. She even gave him a gift like you."

"Yeah, I saw. I think it was his tea reading predictions from the other day." I reached to the mantel and disentangled the carnations Adam had given me from Claudette's lilies. "Mine told me Adam was my soulmate this time." I sniffed at the carnations I'd drawn to me and nestled in my arms. "I'm trying not to get too worked up about it, but I think there really might be something to these readings."

Camille rolled her eyes. Camille didn't believe squat about tea readings.

"You scoff but Claudette was sorta right about some of her first predictions for me. She could be right about the soulmate thing."

"What do you mean?" She reached her hand out. "Let me see your card again."

My eyes did a quick patrol of the room checking for Claudette before passing Camille the box and watching as she removed the card, scanned it, and stowed it away.

"This says nothing about Adam," Camille said.

"Sure it does," I said. "How could you miss it? It's underlined three times. It says: *Soulmate soon in this room* and when I looked up Adam came in. What more proof do you need?"

Camille tucked the box in beside the flowers cradled to me, and we headed for the hall.

"*Mais voyons*, Lora," she said. "That prediction was from yesterday. It had nothing to do with this room. The reading wasn't even in this house."

Hmm, that was true. I looked through the doorway into Claudette's kitchen where Adam, flanked by two women, now grazed at the buffet. Camille was right. Adam hadn't been anywhere near the tea reading. Adam had been at the hospital with Tina when I'd been ambushed with the reading. I frowned. Only two men came into the church kitchen following the reading. Rakeman and Broomman. I shuddered. If Claudette was suggesting either of them was my soulmate she was way off base. Which was a relief in a way because it would disqualify the whole reading and I could forget all about the rest of the predictions.

From the corner of my eye, I spotted Laurent shrugging into his jacket, finally alone and no doubt using the moment to skip out, without so much as any goodbyes to call attention to his exit. I excused myself from Camille for a sec and rushed to catch him before he made his escape.

"Wait up," I said, reaching him on the stoop.

He turned and a gust of wind blew his hair across one eye. He flicked it away and smiled. "You were good tonight in the play, *mon lapin*," he said. "And fast. You made it to your Bunny hole with all your clothes."

"Thanks to you I did. I can't thank you enough for getting me a new costume."

"*De rien.*"

I moved closer and skipped a glance back at the door I'd shut behind me. "Can I ask, why'd you do it? I mean, your aunt was really attached to the first Bunny suit. Weren't you worried she'd be angry?"

Laurent locked eyes with me. "*Tante* Claudette is attached to memories not the suit. She might be upset for a bit, but with time she will see the old one was not right anymore."

I hoped for his sake he was accurate otherwise he'd be courting another finger wag. "Um, can I ask you another question?"

He raised an eyebrow at me that I took as invitation to go ahead.

"Now that it's over, can you tell me what you gave up for Lent?"

He grinned. "It's the cat that is supposed to be curious, not the bunny."

"And that's you avoiding my question. It's only fair you tell me. After all, you know what I gave up."

He nodded. "*Oui*, I do."

"So?"

Our eyes stayed locked but he said nothing, his face still. Not cop face exactly. A stillness I couldn't quite place. Making me wonder if his holding out on me was about more than just privacy. Like maybe it was about me returning the doll he'd given me to the police. Maybe he really was upset with me. Now that I thought about it, he had been less chatty with me since his return from Québec City. Most of our conversations had been confined to required interactions over the bingo money woes. The crack about the cat versus bunny curiosity thing was the first time he'd teased me all week. And maybe that was on reflex. Something that just popped out before he checked himself and now he was shutting down again. Then again, if he was upset with me why had he given me the new Bunny suit? I had to be missing something.

The door opened behind us and Adam came outside. "There you are, Lora. Ready to go?" He swung an arm across my shoulders as his eyes slid briefly to Laurent.

Adam's arm felt heavy on my body but warm, reminding me I'd left my jacket inside.

"Almost," I said in answer to his question. "I just need to grab my coat and say my goodbyes."

"Here," Adam said, moving to release me and pointing to the flowers. "Let me take these while you run back in. When you're done, we can go home and get started on the long weekend."

With everything going on I'd nearly forgotten about the long weekend we'd planned, but with Tina and co heading to their nest and the play behind me, Adam and I really could get on with our own holiday festivities.

Of course, if I left now probably I'd never know what Laurent had given up for Lent. Or if Claudette's finger wag had been warranted. By Tuesday when we got back to work, Easter and all talk of it would be over along with my chance at getting Laurent to crack and spill his secrets. But I couldn't very well press him about them now in front of Adam.

Laurent nodded a goodbye and turned to leave, and I cast a downward glance, briefly wishing I had pickpocket talents. Which got me wondering if my curiosity meter *may* need a few adjustments. It may not qualify as an addition to the deadly sin list, but it could definitely lead me to trouble.

In my moment of distraction, my grip on the carnations loosened, and Adam lifted them to him, allowing Claudette's gift box and the chocolate wrapper to spill out of my arms and hit the stoop.

From the sidewalk, Laurent glanced back and watched as I scooped them up, gripping one in each hand. From his pocket, he pulled out his own gift box and tipped it at me, like a salute.

"*À dimanche*," he said with the hint of a smile. "See you then, Easter rabbit."

I brightened. *Until Sunday*. That was right, I still had Easter Bunny duties at the egg hunt for the kids. I smiled back and waved, thinking maybe I hadn't lost my chance at finding out his secrets. And maybe I wouldn't try to rein in my curiosity just yet.

ACKNOWLEDGMENTS

For me, Easter has always been the holiday with a touch of magic. I mean, bunnies delivering chocolates—how much more magical can it get?

So when I set out to write an Easter story for Lora, I wanted it to have a little touch of magic Lora style. The story unfolded from there with lots of family and community thrown in. Somehow, that also meant that what began as a mini-mystery grew and ended up much longer, and then through a series of unforeseen events, also took longer to come out than planned.

I thank all you readers who stuck with me through the wait. You rock:)

I also thank my family for all the Easter memories that made me want to write about this special holiday.

And, of course, huge thanks to Maud L, the absolute best French editor I could dream of working with who always brings her own magic to the Lora Weaver world.

I feel blessed and lucky to have such an amazing community supporting Lora. And to have the talented Vanessa Labrie narrating the audiobooks for the series and helping celebrate our beloved city of Montréal.

Merci à tous:)

ABOUT THE AUTHOR

Katy Leen is the author of the Lora Weaver mystery novels. She credits her mom for sparking her lifelong love of stories through her own avid love of books. When she's not writing, Katy can be found listening to bookish and wellness podcasts, playing word games, reading, or hanging out with her hubby and family—always with a pup at her side and a cup of cocoa nearby.

Join Katy's *Nouvelles* newsletter where she shares more meanderings and insider info about the books:)

Pop by katyleen.com to check out the Q&A and her blog or Follow Katy at:

ALSO BY KATY LEEN

Lora Weaver Series in Order

The First Faux Pas

The Nearly Nixed Noël (holiday novella)

The Pas de Deux

The Lost Love Liaison (Valentine novella)

The Ménage à Trois

The Easter Egg Ennui (Easter novella)

The Petit-Four Score

More Books

The Demi-Tasse Début (prequel novella)

The Bonne Année Brouhaha (New Year's novella)

The Lora Weaver Bundle

The Lora Weaver Holiday Boxed Set

The Lora Weaver series is still growing! Pop over to my website for news about the latest books.

The series is available in print, ebook, and audiobook.

I hope you join me for more of Lora's adventures:)

Happy reading!

www.ingramcontent.com/pod-product-compliance
Lightning Source LLC
Chambersburg PA
CBHW051245170626
46809CB00004B/1503